JAN 1 4 2022

W9-BQY-659

Next Door to Happy

Next Door to Happy

ALLISON WEISER STROUT

MARGARET FERGUSON BOOKS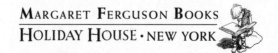
HOLIDAY HOUSE · NEW YORK

Margaret Ferguson Books

HOLIDAY HOUSE is registered in the U.S. Patent and Trademark Office.
Printed and bound in March 2022 at Maple Press, York, PA, USA.
www.holidayhouse.com
First Edition
10 9 8 7 6 5 4 3 2 1

Library of Congress Cataloging-in-Publication Data

Names: Strout, Allison Weiser, author.
Title: Next door to happy / Allison Weiser Strout.
Description: First edition. | New York City : Holiday House, [2022]
   Margaret Ferguson Books. | Audience: Ages 9 to 12. | Audience: Grades
   4–6. | Summary: 12-year-old Violet Crane is an only child in a lonely
   household who longs to be part of the large gregarious family that's just
   moved in next door.
Identifiers: LCCN 2021036041 | ISBN 9780823450862 (hardcover)
Subjects: LCSH: Only child—Juvenile fiction. | Single-parent
   families—Juvenile fiction. | Mothers and daughters—Juvenile fiction.
   Neighbors—Juvenile fiction. | Brothers and sisters—Juvenile fiction.
   Families—Juvenile fiction. | Friendship—Juvenile fiction. | CYAC: Only
   child—Fiction. | Single-parent families—Fiction. | Mothers and
   daughters—Fiction. | Neighbors—Fiction. | Brothers and
   sisters—Fiction. | Family life—Fiction. | Friendship—Fiction.
Classification: LCC PZ7.1.S79725 Ne 2022 | DDC 813/.6 [Fic]—dc23
LC record available at https://lccn.loc.gov/2021036041

ISBN: 978-0-8234-5086-2 (hardcover)

For my mother

Next Door to Happy

One

EVER since they moved in next door last week, I've sat on our front porch watching them. They're out in their yard all day long—laughing and screaming and playing with each other—until their mother calls them in. So far as I can tell, they're a real family. Which means they're the opposite of mine.

This morning the kids are in the yard again. There are five of them—two boys, three girls—and they have divided themselves into two uneven teams for relay races. The kids at the front of the lines crabwalk across the lawn and onto the driveway, where they each bounce a soccer ball once on one knee before hopscotching back across the grass to tag their teammate's hand. A yellow dog stands on the lawn next to them, barking as they cheer one another on.

Every minute I sit here, I want to be there even more. It's been a long summer. I spent the first part as a counselor-in-training at my old day camp, and now my best friend,

Katie Patterson, is at sleepaway camp. My heart is crazy with desire, which is just the kind of emotion that my dad tells me I should try to tone down.

It's been almost a year since he moved out, and at first, I was pretty upset about his leaving, but there were some good things about it. For one, he bought me a phone so that I could call him regularly. Every Wednesday and Saturday I spent the night at his apartment, and we went out to eat at the diner. He would always get the day's special like veal shank or stuffed cabbage, which kind of grossed me out, and I would get some pasta dish. After we ate, we would go back to his place. He let me sleep in the bedroom while he took the fold-out couch in the living room.

But in June he got a job at a different company and started flying from New York to Atlanta every Monday and coming back on Friday, and now I only see him on Saturdays.

Dad's always telling me how he thinks I need to realize that life isn't perfect. It makes me kind of angry because if anyone knows that life isn't perfect, it's me. Maybe he should be telling me instead to grab the chance to be really happy when I get it.

Which is exactly what I'm going to do right now. When I watch those kids play, I can picture being happy just like them. I put on my sneakers and drag my old silver bike out of the garage. I ride up and down our driveway doing careful circles again and again, hoping they'll notice me. The whole time, my eyes are glued to their yard. I crane my neck extra hard so that I can see who is winning.

"You can do it, Reggie," the older boy yells at his brother as he crabwalks across the yard.

"Go, go!" one girl shouts at her sister.

Their dog joins the race, sprinting next to the kids. When the dog comes to the end of the driveway, it starts to tear through the narrow strip of trees between our houses.

"No, Goldie!" one kid shouts.

"Goldie, stop!" screams another.

Suddenly, I am heading straight into a big yellow mound of fur that is right in front of my wheel. The dog veers to the right as I slam on the brakes and close my eyes. My body flies forward, and I fall onto the driveway, making contact with the blacktop. I end up flat on my back, elbows burning. I stay there for a couple of minutes with my eyes scrunched shut. I don't want to get up. I don't want to move.

"Sorry, Goldie doesn't usually run like that," someone says. "Are you all right?"

I open my eyes and stare into the eyes of the older boy. He has shaggy brown hair and a big mouthful of white teeth, and he looks like he's in high school. Boys that age don't usually talk to kids my age.

His team—a younger boy and a little girl—peer at me.

"I'm okay," I say as I tentatively straighten out my bruised elbows and sit up.

"Yeah, TJ. She's fine," says the little girl. "Can we go back to the game now? We were winning."

"Be quiet, Chloe," TJ says. Then he asks me, "Can you stand?"

The younger boy, who still hasn't said one word, sticks his hand out to help me up.

It's kind of embarrassing taking his hand, but it would be even more embarrassing not to take it. His hand is big, and I feel rough calluses on his palm as he gently pulls.

"Are your parents home?" asks TJ. "Do you want me to get them?"

"Really, I'm fine," I say, which is only true if *fine* actually means that your entire body throbs like it's on fire.

"Sorry about Goldie," TJ says. "My mom told me to tie her up, but with all of us outside I didn't think she'd take off. My name's TJ Walker. Do you want to come over? Do you have any brothers or sisters? Maybe they want to come, too?"

"No, it's just me," I say.

"So, do you want to come over?" he asks again.

In my head I'm shouting *Yes, yes, yes*, but I try to play it cool, as if joining their game had never crossed my mind.

"All right," I say.

The three of us take Goldie's path. The silent brother grabs Goldie by the collar and goes first with Chloe following close behind. TJ gestures at me to go after her, and then he takes up the rear as we proceed single file.

When we get to the Walkers' yard, the two other sisters are passing the soccer ball back and forth.

"She's going to play, too," TJ says.

"Okay," the girls say in unison, barely looking up from their practice.

"I forgot to ask you your name," TJ says.

"Violet," I say. "Violet Crane, from, uh, next door."

The two sisters look at each other and giggle. Even the corner of the silent boy's mouth turns up a little. I guess they know I'm from next door, but it's really not *that* funny.

"Get out of here!" TJ exclaims.

"I'm Rose," says the girl in the blue T-shirt, who's still got the soccer ball between her feet. She's got dirty-blond hair that's pulled back in a high ponytail, and she wears a sweatband that matches her shirt. She has tan, muscular legs.

"And I'm Daisy," says the one with two golden braids and a calm expression on her face. She's about the same height as her sister, but everything about her is stick-like: her arms, her legs. Even her face is long and narrow.

"Our parents picked their names because when they were born, Rose was bright red and Daisy came out white as a sheet," says TJ. "Now the rest of us are stuck explaining their flowery names all the time. But how do we explain this? Rose, Daisy, and *Violet*!"

"Were you purple when you came out?" Chloe asks.

"Chloe!" Rose says. "Don't mind her—and obviously, you have to be on our team now."

"Definitely," Daisy agrees. Her voice is sweeter than her sister's.

I think I should say something peppy and enthusiastic— something to match the twins' level of enthusiasm—but I'm the kind of person who comes up with the right thing to say about twenty minutes after the moment to say the right thing has passed. And as usual, nothing comes to mind now, even though I am seriously excited to be part of their team.

At home, when my parents were still together, we were never a team. There was my father, who was usually angry, and my mother, who was lost in her own problems. For as long as I can remember, my mom has preferred staying home to going out, but as her anxieties got worse over the last few years, she left the house less and less, and that made my father mad. She got more and more nervous about going to parties or school events—she didn't even like to have to make conversation with other parents when she walked me to the bus stop. When she does have to talk to people she doesn't know, she always acts weird. It's embarrassing. She saw a doctor who tried to help her, but she got frustrated and gave up. That's a big part of why my father left—he thought she should work harder to get over her problems.

"It'll be me, Reggie, and Chloe against Violet, Rose, and Daisy. Who wants to show Violet what to do?" TJ asks.

"I will," Chloe says, pushing the curls away from her face and balling up her fists in concentration. "Of course, you're not going to be able to go as fast as I do. I have the record."

"Okay, Chloe, we get it," says Rose. She lightly taps the soccer ball as we follow Chloe back to the beginning of the course. "How old are you, anyway?"

"Twelve," I say. "I graduated from sixth grade, which means I'm starting middle school this year."

"In our old district, sixth grade *was* middle school," complains Rose. "Now because our father got a new job and we had to move here, we're stuck in elementary school for another year. So unfair. Right, Dais?"

Daisy nods.

"Violet's in your grade, Reg," adds Rose.

While we've been talking, Reggie's sat down. He's plucking blades of grass from the lawn, and instead of responding to Rose, he holds a blade to his mouth and makes a whistling noise.

"Reggie doesn't like school," says Chloe.

"Shhh, Chloe," says Daisy.

"That's okay," I say. "Lots of people don't."

Even to my ears that sounds kind of lame. I should be agreeable and say what everybody says—I don't like school either. But the fact is, I actually don't mind school. At school, no one's family is there.

"Let's go, guys," says TJ. "Back to the races."

Reggie gets up, and we split into teams and do relays for a couple of hours. It turns out that I'm a pretty fast crabwalker, so I help our team a lot. We flower girls win three out of four races, and when we're done playing, Rose throws her arm around Daisy and the two of them start doing a kickline to celebrate. Then Rose throws her other arm around me and makes me do the dance, too.

❋❋❋❋❋❋❋❋❋❋❋

"Only five minutes to change classes?" my mother asks that night when she reads from the Benjamin Franklin Middle

School official welcome package that arrived in the mail today. School starts in two weeks. My schedule says that homeroom is from 8:30 to 8:45 in Room B-116. Then I have math from 8:50 to 9:35 and gym 9:40 to 10:25 and so on and so on until the day is over.

"I hope you can find your way around," she says.

"I'll be fine."

"I'm sure you will be. I did well in school, too," she says.

My mother likes to point out how there was a time in her life when she used to act the same as everyone else. Even though she tended to be shy, she had a normal life. She got out and went places and did things with friends. She thinks it will make me feel better, knowing that she hasn't always been the way she is now, but actually it only makes me feel worse. I just wish she could be like other moms.

Two

SINCE that first day, the Walker kids always expect me to come over to their yard and play with them. Most of the time they are already outside by the time I finish breakfast. They are all early risers, except for Rose, who, according to Daisy, needs to be rousted out of bed every single day by her sister.

"Nobody else will do it because she once punched TJ in the face by accident when she was waking up," says Daisy. "She dreams a lot."

"Yeah, it's true," says Rose. "Even Mom won't come near me. She just stands at the door and rings a little bell. I don't want to get up because I'm having a really good dream and you guys interrupt it. Like today, I was dreaming about how I scored this incredible goal at soccer tryouts. Daisy kicked the ball to me, and I planted it in the back of the net. One touch. Boom. Goalie didn't know what happened."

"Let's see about that now," says TJ. "I'll be the goalie, and this time Violet and Reggie are on my team. You flower girls need to be broken up."

"Chloe, that means you're on our team," says Rose. "You can be our goalie."

"You are so lucky," says Chloe. "I'm very good. Ms. McMann said so."

"Yeah, right," says Rose. "We're *so* lucky."

"You *are*, Rose. Don't make fun of me," says Chloe.

"Don't worry about it, Chloe," says Daisy. "Right, Violet?"

"Right," I say, happy to agree. Daisy isn't the twin you notice first, but it's hard not to like her. "Chloe, do you want me to put your hair in French braids so it's off your face and you can see better?" I may not be a star on the soccer field, but I'm pretty good with my hands, so all kinds of crafty things come easily to me. Plus, when I was little, I had a doll that had a big clump of red hair, and I became an expert in coming up with new hairstyles, including making all kinds of fancy braids.

Chloe nods at me, so I sit behind her and divide her hair into two equal sections. She stays perfectly still as I carefully braid each side.

"Someone needs to go get Reggie if we're going to play. He's out in the back again," says Daisy.

"Violet, why don't you go?" says TJ. "He'll pay more attention to you than any of us."

After I finish Chloe's braids, I head to the backyard to find Reggie. He's not like Daisy or Rose—always with a soccer ball between their feet, constantly pushing it around and defending themselves against imaginary opponents. If Reggie's not playing with his siblings, he's off by himself, looking for birds. He has a guidebook that identifies all of the birds of the Northeast, and he wants to spot every single species before he finishes middle school. He's been able to check a whole bunch of new birds off his list, and he says it's been the best thing so far about moving to a new place.

"Hey, Violet, look," says Reggie, who is standing so close to a bush that he looks like he's a part of it. "Do you see?"

I position myself next to him and stare straight ahead, but all I can make out is a tangled network of branches and leaves.

"To the right. I think it's an abandoned finch's nest."

I turn my head just a little and squint hard. Now that I know where it is, I can spot a neat structure of twigs and grass resting on one of the branches.

"Wow, cool. How did you know it was here?" I ask.

"When we first moved in I kept seeing the same bird hanging around on the ground over here. It would fly around right there and then every once in a while it would sneak inside the bush. I think it was feeding its babies. You can see five hatched eggs still in there."

"Five, just like you guys," I say, suddenly remembering that I was actually sent here on official business. "Everybody wants you to come play soccer. We're going to start a game, and this time it's going to be you and me and TJ against everyone else."

TJ is right about Reggie listening to me. He takes one last look at the nest and follows me back to the front yard, where Chloe has already planted herself in one of the goals.

"Yay, now we can finally play," says Rose.

"We're going to beat you!" Chloe yells from her spot in the goal, her voice sounding particularly loud since we've just come from the quiet of the backyard.

The Walkers have a good lawn for soccer—wide and flat. The only problem is the giant oak tree planted smack in the middle that makes a weird dividing line right through everything.

I am going head-to-head against Daisy in this game, and Reggie takes Rose.

"Okay, face off," shouts TJ from his goalie position.

Reggie and Rose both take aim at the ball. Rose focuses in like she is going to clobber it, sending it straight to TJ in the goal, but at the last second Reggie's foot touches the ball and gently redirects it, so it rolls ten feet in front of me. I run hard to reach it before Daisy gets it.

From the corner of my eye, I can see Chloe jumping up and down in her goal.

"Get it, Daisy!" Chloe shouts.

I try to kick the ball, but Daisy taps it expertly in Rose's direction. Then Rose gets control and runs straight toward TJ with Reggie right beside her. She manages to keep Reggie away with her footwork, then takes aim. It is a beautiful, solid kick, but TJ sticks his arms out and easily catches the ball and flings it right at me.

"Go, Violet, go!" he says.

I trap the ball with my feet. Oh my God, did one of those drills from gym class actually work? That has to be a first. Here I am playing in an actual game with actual friends (can I call them friends?) and I am not embarrassing myself.

"Violet, Violet, I'm here," Reggie says.

I glance down at my feet to make sure I am set up for the shot—and *bam*. It is like my head explodes.

I am flat on my back with TJ peering over me. Again. Actually, this time all five of the Walkers circle around, looking at me.

"Isn't it our ball because she ran into the tree?" asks Chloe.

"Shut up, Chloe," TJ says.

"Mom says you shouldn't say that to me. It's not nice," says Chloe.

"Are you okay?" asks Reggie.

"Can you stand up?" asks Rose.

"I think I'm all right. Really." I guess it's true. I put my hands up to my face to check for dripping blood. There's no blood, but I can feel a big bump forming on my forehead, and the world is spinning a little bit.

"She needs to go inside," Reggie says. He looks really concerned—more concerned than everyone else huddled around me. "Mom should look at her." Then he turns to me and says, "Our mom used to be a nurse."

"I guess," says TJ, but he doesn't seem thrilled about the idea. Even though it wasn't his fault, I get the feeling that he's used to getting the blame when things go wrong.

"Really, I feel okay," I say, standing up.

Rose ignores me, grabs my hand, and leads me toward the house. On the front porch is a striped straw welcome mat and a big round planter filled with purple flowers. As Daisy and TJ head in before us, they both quickly wipe their feet on the mat. I wipe, too.

"Don't worry about it," says Rose. "There are exceptions made for those with injuries."

I wipe my dirty sneakers again anyway.

"Mom!" TJ shouts, leading us through an entryway with a big mirror and one of those old-fashioned coatracks, a raincoat and two soccer jackets hanging off its arms. Underneath our feet is a soft rug.

"She's probably in the kitchen," says Rose.

The Walkers moved in less than two weeks ago, but their house is already organized. We pass through the living room, which has a comfortable-looking beige sofa, a bright turquoise armchair, and plants, lots and lots of plants. There is a chaise lounge in the corner that looks inviting. One of the kids must have been sitting there recently, because a big book of comics sits open on top of a nubby plaid throw.

In the kitchen, shiny brass pots and saucepans hang on the wall. On the table is a clear glass bowl filled with water and a few pink flowers floating on top. Mrs. Walker has her back to us, stirring something on the stove.

"What did I tell you? Back door, back door!"

"Sorry, kind of an emergency," says TJ.

"Oh, no," Mrs. Walker says, flipping around to see me holding my hand over my forehead. "You're Violet?"

I nod.

"What have you guys done to her? First Goldie runs her over, and now what?"

No one says anything. I'm a little worried because it doesn't seem likely that Mrs. Walker will want me around if I am winning the Most Accident-Prone Kid of the Neighborhood Award. At the same time, I feel weirdly happy that they must have mentioned me before. By name.

"It's not our fault," says Chloe. "*She* ran into the tree."

"Chlo-eee," say Daisy and Rose together.

"Well, she did. Violet's clumsy," says Chloe.

"I guess I am," I say, trying to be agreeable.

"It's not Violet's fault. The front yard is just not that great for sports. Maybe we should cut the tree down," says Rose, clearly trying to advance her own soccer-playing agenda.

"No! I like that tree!" says Chloe. "I'm going to learn to climb it like Reggie did yesterday. He got to the very top."

"You did what?" says Mrs. Walker to Reggie. "What did I tell you?"

"He was probably talking to the squirrels again," says Chloe.

"Reggie!" says Mrs. Walker.

Reggie doesn't say anything but turns to Chloe with his lips pressed together and his eyes narrowed.

"Let's take a look at you," Mrs. Walker says to me. "TJ, did it seem like she blacked out?"

"No. Definitely not."

"That's quite a bump," says Mrs. Walter. Then she reaches into a cabinet for a first-aid bag and pulls out a light, like the kind a doctor uses to check your throat.

"Follow this with your eyes. Any nausea? Are you lightheaded?"

I shake my head twice. "Really, I'm fine. It was just kind of a surprise."

"I bet it was," she says. "Let's at least get you some ice for that bump. Is your mother home? We should tell her so she can keep an eye on you."

"She's at home," I say. *She's almost always at home,* I think.

"Great. I can introduce myself at the same time," says Mrs. Walker.

"It's all right," I protest. "I'll go home and tell her. You don't have to come with me."

"I'd like to meet your mother," says Mrs. Walker kindly, "now that we're neighbors."

Should I tell Mrs. Walker that my mother isn't looking for new friends? Her friends are people she's known forever, and she's not even completely honest with them about her problems. That's the worst part about her anxieties: she doesn't want anyone to find out about them. And the possibility that someone might makes her avoid meeting new people even more.

But, of course, I can't say any of that. Instead, I try to come up with an excuse that makes sense.

"She works at home, so it's not always a good time," I say.

"Well, I wouldn't want to disturb her," says Mrs. Walker. "Why don't you ask her when would be a good time for me to come over? Or, of course, she's welcome to stop by here anytime. A few of the other neighbors already have."

"I'm sure she'd love that," I lie.

▪▪▪▪▪▪▪▪▪▪▪▪▪

When I get home from the Walkers', my mother is sitting on her bed in stretchy black pants and a shapeless white shirt, a stack of papers in her lap. She works freelance, writing advertising copy for a lot of different companies. She has a small computer desk in the corner of the room, but she usually does her work on her bed, propped up by a stack of pillows.

I am still holding the ice wrapped in a blue towel against my forehead.

"Oh, Violet, what happened?" she asks.

"I ran into a tree when we were playing," I explain. "I'm okay, but Mrs. Walker says you need to look for any unusual behavior in the next twenty-four hours."

"Who's Mrs. Walker? And how does she know what I need to do?" asks my mother.

"She's our new neighbor next door. She used to be a nurse, so she knows. Also, she says she wants to come over to meet you."

The minute I mention this, I wish I hadn't.

"She does? Why?"

"Isn't that what neighbors do?" I ask.

"Oh, did she say that?"

"No, she didn't." In a way, Mrs. Walker did say that, but not how my mother is suggesting, so I add, "I think she was just being nice." I take the towel off my head and ball it up in my hands.

"All that matters is that you're okay now. What were you doing when you bumped your head?"

"Playing soccer," I say, noticing that the melting ice is starting to drip onto the floor. "There are five kids, so we can play a pretty good game."

"Five kids? That's a lot. Maybe they're too rough for you."

"They're not rough. I just ran into a tree because I was looking down at the ball. It could happen to anyone."

"But it never happened to you before," she insists.

"That's because since my job ended at Lanford Day Camp I'm inside, drawing or reading. How could I run into a tree doing that? Anyway, I like having kids to play with."

Before the Walkers moved in, there was only one other kid my age in our neighborhood—Owen Simon, whom I don't have anything in common with.

"What about Katie?" my mother asks.

"She's on vacation. Reggie, one of the kids next door, is in my grade at school," I say, putting the towel down on my mother's desk chair.

I allow myself to daydream for a second. Maybe if it's so easy for me to be comfortable with the Walkers, my mother would be comfortable, too.

"You could try going over there to meet them," I say. "Or invite Mrs. Walker here."

"I could, but right now I have a deadline."

"What about later?"

"Maybe later," she says.

I know from experience that *later* never happens.

:::::::::::

I've never heard one of the Walker kids make excuses for their mom—probably because she's so perfect—like I have to make for my mom.

I'm not good at coming up with excuses when they're just about me. Kids at school tell all kinds of dumb lies when they forget their homework, but I can't seem to do it. Last year, one boy in my class told our teacher that he had held his homework out the bus window and it blew away—although that excuse was so stupid maybe it was true. When I forget my homework, I sit there silently until the teacher figures it out and tells me not to let it happen again.

But when it comes to my mother, I am a champion excuse maker. I can tell big lies and little lies. I know how to bite my tongue and hold in all kinds of things. When my teacher asked if my mother might be available to chaperone a field trip, I said she couldn't change her work schedule that day. When Katie wanted to know if my mother was going to be at the annual schoolwide spelling bee, I told her that she had the flu and wouldn't be better by then. Mom does make an effort when Katie comes to my house, but that doesn't happen very often—I usually go to Katie's house. I wish I could tell Katie the truth about my mother, but it feels like a secret and I'm not sure she would understand.

Last year a new girl, Missy Edwards, moved to our town. I was jealous because her mother and Katie's mother got together all the time. They took Katie and Missy shopping and out to eat. Their two families even went to California on spring break, and when Katie and Missy came back to school they wore matching San Diego Zoo T-shirts and braided necklaces with little silver dolphins from Sea World.

The last time I was at Katie's house was before summer vacation started, and she had invited Missy over, too. Missy had been at Katie's so much that she opened the big walnut cabinets in the kitchen looking for cookies as if she lived there herself. No matter what the three of us did at Katie's house, I felt like I was tagging along. Even the next day when we were eating lunch in the cafeteria, Katie and Missy only talked about things they'd done after I'd gone home, and how much they were looking forward to being at sleepaway camp together.

When I got home from school, I tried to explain it to my mother.

"That's how kids are," she said, looking up from her computer. "Find somebody else to sit with."

"It's not that easy. I always eat lunch with Katie."

"You should make new friends anyway," she said.

I could tell she wasn't really listening to me, so I took out my sketchbook and pencils and started to doodle.

"I'm just trying to help you," she added.

If my mom really wanted to help me, she'd make an effort to do things with Katie's mom. She'd go over and meet Mrs. Walker.

 Three

THE next day it pours, so I know the Walker kids won't be outside. I actually don't mind being home today—in the rain, our house always seems a little cozier than when it's nice out. I pull on my oldest black leggings and a comfortable hoodie. My mother's still sleeping, so I sneak into her room and climb onto the bed on my father's side. I pick up one of the pencils and a piece of paper from the supplies I keep on his nightstand and start to draw my mother. I try to capture the peaceful look on her face as she sleeps, but it's not easy. So much of people's expressions are in their eyes that it's tricky to get their face right if they're closed. After I make a couple of attempts, I start to get hungry, so I grab some more paper and the pencils and head to the kitchen.

The kitchen is the nicest room in the house—not because of the furniture but because it has big picture windows that look out into the woods behind the house. An uneven stone wall runs through the woods, stretching through the backyards of all of the houses on my street. According to my fourth-grade teacher, the walls were built by farmers hundreds of years ago and were used for cover by Revolutionary War soldiers when they were shooting at British soldiers.

Katie has a great-great-great-great-great-grandfather who fought in that war. She lives about twenty minutes away from here in a big white house with wooden shingles that has been in her family for generations. It has low ceilings and slate floors, and the front hallway is lined with silver-framed photos of old relatives.

The only framed photo that we have in our house is one my mother has on her nightstand. In the picture, I'm about three years old, and I'm in motion, my arms spread out like a bird's wings. My mother says that my arms are open because I'm barreling toward her about to give her a big hug. She says that's why the picture is so special.

Sometimes I hold the picture and try to remember what I was actually doing when it was taken, and I don't think my mother is completely right. I might have been running to her, but I'm pretty sure that I was imagining I could fly. The photo had caught me just as I was pretending to soar high in the sky—above her and my father and our house.

After I eat a bowl of cereal, I pick up a gray pencil and start to draw a picture of our house. First, I visualize it, and then I begin to sketch, getting the basic shape down before adding the details in color. Even though no one has ever really taught me how to draw, last year my art teacher was always holding up my pictures in front of the class and telling everyone to notice the way I used perspective—which according to her is just making everything look right from the viewer's eye.

I'm working on the finishing touches when I hear footsteps on the porch, and then a knock.

I put down my drawing and run to answer it.

"Who is it?" I ask with the door closed.

"Rose."

"And Daisy."

I open the door and the twins are standing on the porch, both in yellow raincoats. Their hoods must have come off when they were running over, because their hair is sopping wet. Beyond the cover of the porch, the rain is really coming down.

"Our mom says you can come over this afternoon," says Rose.

"And stay for dinner. We're having lasagna," adds Daisy.

"If your mother says it's okay, you can come any time after lunch," says Rose, before turning to Daisy. "Beat you home."

"I'm sure it's okay!" I shout after them as they vault off the porch.

Daisy is in the lead, but just before they get to Goldie's path, Rose grabs her sister's arm to slow her down and pulls ahead.

I go to my mom's room and open the door a crack. "Mom," I whisper.

"Violet, please," she says, opening one eye. She's still in bed and has an old patchwork quilt pulled up to her chin.

"The Walkers invited me over this afternoon. And they said I could stay for dinner."

"Is it someone's birthday or something?"

"I don't think so. They just invited me. They're having lasagna."

She sighs and pushes her arms against the bed so she's sitting up. Then she leans her head against the wall and closes her eyes for a second as if she's going back to sleep. When she opens them again, she says, "Okay, but you have to tell me all about it when you come home."

"Thanks, Mom," I say, going in and kissing her on the cheek.

She pulls me in closer and hugs me. "Have fun. Can you please close my door on the way out?"

I wait in the living room thinking about what time "after lunch" means. I don't want to interrupt the Walkers in the middle of their meal. They'll probably be having grilled cheese and tomato soup or something cozy like that. That's definitely what people who make lasagna for dinner have for lunch. The whole group probably sits around the table and talks and laughs.

I decide I can go to the Walkers' house around 1:30. I get my drawing from the kitchen and continue to work on it, holding it out at arm's length to admire it. I might not have gotten every detail right, but you would definitely know it's our house by looking at it. Then I draw a picture of all of us playing soccer for Rose and Daisy—and one more picture for Chloe because she'll probably complain if she doesn't get one, too. When it's time to go, I roll the two pictures up and stick them under my shirt so they don't get wet. Then I grab my raincoat and shout goodbye loudly so my mother knows I'm leaving.

It is only raining a little now. I walk slowly up our driveway and across Goldie's path.

I pause a few feet from the house because I can't decide which door to use. Mrs. Walker had been angry when we came in through the front entrance after I had banged my head, and since my sneakers are muddy, I walk past the house, around the garage, and through the backyard just like I've seen the Walker kids do. There's a big boulder right in the middle of the backyard; it looks the same as one of the rocks from the stone wall behind our houses but a thousand times bigger. Three large crows stand bunched up on a flat part at the top of the rock, dipping their feet into an hourglass-shaped puddle of water that has formed from the rain.

There's also a picnic table and a scattering of white wooden chairs. Reggie is perched on the edge of one of them, facing the rock. He's wearing a navy-blue raincoat, the hood pulled tight against his head, and tall professional-looking rainboots, like the kind fishermen would use. The rest of the Walkers must be inside.

Reggie turns around when he hears me.

"You're here," he says.

"Yeah," I say. "Rose and Daisy invited me. For the afternoon and dinner."

"I know. I was waiting for you."

"Out here in the rain?"

"It's better than inside. My mother is on a cleaning rampage, and I needed an escape. Believe me, you're better off out here," he says, pointing at the chair next to him.

I sit down on the edge of it, pulling my raincoat underneath me so I don't get my jeans wet. The pictures I drew for the Walkers are still under my shirt. I would rather go inside and be dry, but it seems like it would be rude to leave Reggie on his own.

"What are you doing?" I say.

"Just looking at them," he says, pointing at the crows.

"Looking at them do what?"

"I don't know. Watching them with one another, I guess."

"Oh," I say, and I watch the crows, too. They're actually pretty entertaining; they look like they're having a good time in their makeshift birdbath. First, they dip their feet into the water and then one by one they put their heads down and stick their beaks in, too.

"Sometimes they dip their food in water to soften it up," he explains. "Crows are really smart. With some kinds of puzzles, they can be as smart as a seven-year-old kid."

"So, they're as smart as Chloe?" I ask.

"And way less annoying," he says with a laugh. "They even recognize human faces."

"That's crazy," I say. "Do they know your face?"

"I don't think so. They mostly only remember you if you've upset them."

We sit for a while longer watching the birds, but then the rain really starts to come down again. The birds don't seem to care, but I hold the collar of my raincoat up around my neck.

"You're getting pretty wet," Reggie says. "We should probably go in."

He gets up from his chair and I follow. He pushes the back door open, and Goldie comes running to greet us. She sniffs a little at me, but mostly she seems excited to have Reggie back inside. I get the feeling that Reggie is Goldie's favorite person in the family.

"Violet's here! Can we start the game now?" Chloe shouts from the kitchen.

"Let her come in first," says Mrs. Walker. "Just leave your shoes and coat in here," she says to me, poking her head into the mudroom. "Reggie, make sure that back door is closed so Goldie doesn't get out."

The mudroom is a large hallway off the kitchen lined with painted wooden cubbies that seem to be arranged in order from smallest to biggest, with Chloe's holding yellow rain boots with bumblebee stripes on one end and Mr. and Mrs. Walkers' sturdy hiking boots at the other end. Next to the cubbies stands a ceramic cylinder filled with umbrellas. On the other wall hangs an assortment of racquets, lacrosse sticks, and baseball bats, and there's a red plastic tub in the corner filled with soccer balls.

Reggie puts his raincoat on a hook, and so do I. Then Reggie takes off his boots and leans them against the wall, and I kick my wet sneakers off next to them. I get the rolled-up pictures out from under my shirt and hold them in my hand.

Looking down, I see I have on one blue sock and one brown sock. I think the brown one is my mother's, judging from the extra bunch of material at the toes.

"We're going to play hide-and-seek," he says. "Hope that's okay."

It's nice that Reggie cares, but I can't imagine rejecting any game they want to play. Monkey in the middle, dodgeball—keep the ball away from me or slam me with it—I wouldn't care right now. I'd do it with the Walkers.

We go into the kitchen and Chloe points to the paper rolls in my hand and says, "What's that?"

"Pictures," I say. "I drew them this morning for you guys."

"Cool!" Daisy takes them and shows Mrs. Walker my work. "Look, Mom."

"Aren't those fantastic," says Mrs. Walker, taking the pictures from Daisy. "We can put them up on the corkboard."

"C'mon, let's start the game already!" says Chloe, jumping up and down. "Walker girls against the rest of you!"

"Chlo-eee," Daisy says softly.

"What?"

"Geez, Chloe," Rose says. "What Daisy is trying to say is maybe that's not so nice to Violet."

Chloe crosses her arms in front of her and makes a sour face.

"It's fine," TJ says. "Violet wants to be on my and Reggie's team anyway. Right, Violet?"

"Sure," I say.

"Listen, you guys, I don't want to hear any fighting today. If there are any problems, go to TJ," says Mrs. Walker. "He's in charge."

"That's not fair. Why is he in charge?" asks Rose.

"He's in charge because I'm paying him to be in charge. He's the official babysitter. I need to get a few things done around here."

"I don't need a babysitter," says Chloe.

"Don't you get that *you're* the reason she's stuck paying him?" complains Rose.

"No I'm not. Am I, Mom?"

"No," says Mrs. Walker, giving Rose a look as she walks out of the kitchen. "He's just good at organizing games."

"We're going to crush you guys," says TJ.

"No you're not. *We* are going to crush *you!*" says Chloe.

"Best two out of three," TJ says. "Losers set the table for a week and do the dishes."

"But that isn't fair," says Chloe. "If Violet loses, she can't help with the table or the dishes except for tonight."

Everyone looks at her.

"Wh-what? It's true," says Chloe.

"I guess she's right," I say.

"See," says Chloe. "Violet says I'm right."

"Don't worry about it," says TJ. "There are plenty of us to do the chores without Violet."

We flip a coin to see which team goes first. We win and TJ says, "Team huddle."

He grabs my arm, gestures to Reggie, and we follow him into the dining room. On the long table there are seven piles of clothes and a giant mound of laundry still in the basket. Mrs. Walker picks up a small pink shirt and starts to fold it.

"Don't mind us," TJ says. "We're working on a hide-and-seek strategy."

"Just make sure that strategy doesn't involve hiding behind laundry. Laundry I have just folded. Because if you knock any of those piles over, you'd better have a *real* hiding strategy." She turns to me. "How are you doing, Violet? Is your head feeling better?"

I give her my patented thumbs-up gesture, the one I make when I don't know what else to say.

TJ says, "You guys could hide together if you want, since Violet doesn't know the house, but I'm hiding alone. I've got a great spot in the attic picked out for myself."

"That sounds good to me," I say, and Reggie nods.

"What else?" TJ asks.

"We can hide anywhere but closets," Reggie says quietly.

"Good point," TJ says. "Closets are the most obvious place in the world."

"Got it," I say.

"Ready?"

Reggie and I nod, so TJ shouts to his sisters in the kitchen. "Meeting's over!"

"Give us five," yells Rose.

"I bet she's trying to convince Chloe not to hide in the closets," says TJ. "Good luck with that. Chloe never listens to anyone."

"TJ," says Mrs. Walker.

"C'mon, Mom. We let her play even though she always throws a fit when she loses. And it's always her fault that her team loses anyway."

"She's seven," says Mrs. Walker.

"Did any of the rest of us throw fits like that?"

"She's just trying to keep up," says Mrs. Walker, folding a pair of pants.

"And I'm just trying to warn Violet about what she's in for. She doesn't have any brothers or sisters to put up with."

I can't help staring at TJ and Mrs. Walker going back and forth good-naturedly. Although TJ's smile is like his mother's, he doesn't look much like her. She's fairer than he is, with golden hair, an upturned nose, and narrow eyes, just like the girls. Reggie looks more like TJ. They both have brown eyes and thick, bushy eyebrows. I know that I don't look like any of the Walker girls, but with my fuzzy brown hair and rounder face, I might be able to pass for TJ and Reggie's sister.

"We're ready!" Rose says, coming out of the kitchen with Chloe and Daisy.

"Go back in the kitchen while you count," TJ says. "And don't cheat!"

"I'm sure your sisters wouldn't cheat," says Mrs. Walker.

"Are you kidding? Some of them would." He looks straight at Chloe as she heads for the kitchen.

"I would not," Chloe says.

"TJ, please. I cannot take a whole day of this. Stop baiting her," says Mrs. Walker.

"I was just kidding." He turns to me and Reggie and says, "Let's play," before heading out of the kitchen.

"C'mon," says Reggie. First, we go into the living room, searching for a good hiding spot. It doesn't look promising, so he leads me back through the kitchen, down the hall and up the stairs where there is one large bedroom and two small ones. The large one is the twins'. It's painted purple and has bunk beds and sheer curtains at the window. Next we go by TJ's—his giant sneakers sit in the hallway, and there are posters of baseball players all over the walls. I follow Reggie into Chloe's room, which is neat and tidy and has a four-poster bed with a lacy white comforter.

"Let's hide in here," says Reggie.

"How about behind this chair? I think we can fit if we squeeze in," I say. We both get behind Chloe's enormous beanbag chair, and then arrange the beans into their tallest formation. I already feel so comfortable with Reggie that I don't mind that our arms and legs are squeezed together; from our shoulders to our feet, we're like one person.

"Three, two, one. Here we come!" Chloe shouts.

I hear the three of them going into TJ's room first and then moving in to check the twins' room. From our hiding spot, I watch as they quietly file into Chloe's room. Chloe enters first, going straight to the closet door and throwing it open with a flourish. Rose and Daisy get down on their hands and knees to search under the bed and in the corners. I realize that I'm pressing my arm against Reggie's to keep myself steady, and I'm glad our faces are plastered against the fabric of the chair, because it muffles the sound of our breathing.

"Maybe they're downstairs" says Rose.

"Yeah, let's check there," says Chloe. I feel Reggie's arm shift just a little against mine.

"Wait!" says Daisy. "Look!"

"We found you!" shouts Chloe. "I see Violet's sock!"

I peer down and see that the extra material in the toe of my sock is sticking out beyond the beanbag.

"Sorry," I say to Reggie. "I didn't know."

"I was the one who moved," he says. "Anyway, they still have to find TJ."

●●●●●●●●●●●●

After ten minutes of looking on the first floor, the girls still couldn't find TJ, so we are all back upstairs again.

"Do you guys give up?" asks Reggie.

"Yeah," says Rose. "New game."

"No, we can find him. We can, we can," Chloe says. She pulls on Rose's arm, but Rose ignores her.

"C'mon out, TJ," says Rose. "We give up."

We are crowded together in the hallway. Something above

us creaks and a trapdoor from the ceiling starts to open. TJ sits on the floorboards in the opening above us and unfolds a metal staircase that looks like the bent legs of an insect.

"Watch out," says TJ. "I'm coming down."

When the stairs finally straighten out completely and touch the floor, TJ turns around and starts to climb down.

"Wow!" says Rose.

"Cool," says Daisy.

"No fair!" says Chloe. "No one said he could do that."

"No, but I don't think there's a rule against it," I say, defending TJ. I've already learned a little strategy from Daisy and realize that if I'm going to challenge Chloe, I better quickly follow by changing the subject to distract her, so I add, "What's up there anyway?"

"Not much right now. I heard Mom and Dad say we could use it as a third floor someday. Maybe it could be an extra bedroom," says Rose.

"I want it," says Chloe.

"You already have a room," says Daisy.

"Maybe Reggie will want it," says TJ.

"Reggie has to sleep right across from Mom and Dad," says Chloe. She grins widely as she discloses this piece of information.

"Chloe!" says Daisy.

"I don't think he'd like to sleep up there," says Rose.

Reggie doesn't say a word as his sisters talk about him. I'd like to come to his rescue, but I don't know what to say.

"Our parents will probably force him to stay across from their room forever," says Chloe, spiller of the family secrets. "Mom says he needs a little extra help."

Reggie makes a horrible face at her but still doesn't defend himself.

"Like remember when you had that dream that your bed was moved to the other side of the room and then when you got up in the middle of night you couldn't figure out the way to get out, so you had to call Mom and Dad?" Chloe says to Reggie.

"You can't remember that. You were barely born," says Daisy.

"So?" says Chloe. "Mom told me about it."

"Hello! Can we focus on what we've found here?" Rose says. "That room could be an awesome kids' playroom."

"Yeah! And we could have sleepovers there. Maybe Mom would let us use it tonight and you can sleep over, Violet," says Chloe.

Although I feel like a terrible traitor to Reggie, I can't help but be grateful to Chloe for being so willing to include me. I don't picture Mrs. Walker agreeing to us sleeping in the attic, but maybe she'd let us camp out in the living room. Probably TJ wouldn't want to, but the rest of us could. We could get under a pile of blankets and pillows and stay up really late and tell each other ghost stories. I bet Mrs. Walker would make pancakes in the morning.

"Mom will say no," says Rose.

"Let's ask her," says Chloe.

"Just forget about it," says Daisy.

"You go along with everything Rose says," says Chloe. "I'm going to tell Mom you're being mean to me."

"If you do, you're going to be in so much trouble," says Rose.

"Mom said I was in charge," says TJ, watching the three of them face off. "And I say the round's over, and you guys have to hide now."

"Then *you* have to go in the kitchen! And make sure to count all the way from a hundred," says Chloe.

"We definitely will," I say.

Reggie hasn't looked at me since Chloe told me he slept across from his mom and dad. Maybe he's afraid that since we're going to the same school, I'll blab about the fact that he's scared or something, but I wouldn't do that.

When Reggie and I follow TJ into the kitchen to count, Mrs. Walker is at the sink scrubbing out a pot. Two big pans of lasagna sit on the counter waiting to be put in the oven.

I follow TJ to the table, but Reggie stops and stands by the window.

"Are the crows still out there?" I ask.

Reggie shakes his head. He looks like he would rather be outside even without the birds there.

"How's the game going?" asks Mrs. Walker.

"What do you think? We're playing with Chloe," TJ says.

"Not good?" says Mrs. Walker. "Has she been giving you a hard time, Violet?"

"Not really," I say.

"C'mon, Mom, Violet's not going to be honest," says TJ.

"You have to forgive her. Chloe doesn't understand some-times," Mrs. Walker says to me.

"Are you kidding? She understands *everything*," says TJ. "And whatever you ask her to do, she does the opposite."

Even though Reggie is still staring out the window, he is listening to our conversation, because he turns to grin at TJ.

"When we find her, she'll have a fit and come running to you. C'mon, let's just get this over with," TJ says. "Count loudly. Last time we played, Chloe had a tantrum and said we found her so quickly because she couldn't hear us."

Although he's being kind of mean about Chloe, I think I'd like to have a brother who knew me so well. If I had a brother like TJ, I wouldn't care if he made fun of me or if he won all of the games we played together.

The house is quiet, so we hear it when a door closes shut.

"That's Chloe heading into her closet," says TJ.

Reggie and I crack up.

"Let's not find her," TJ says just before we begin counting. "I'd rather do the dishes every day than have to deal with her."

 # Four

WE lost the rest of the games on purpose, so now TJ, Reggie, and I are setting the table for dinner. Chloe is delirious with happiness.

"Don't forget the napkins," she says. "Right, Mom?"

"Don't gloat," says Mrs. Walker.

"What? You always tell us not to forget the napkins. I'm just reminding them," Chloe says, dancing around the room.

"Violet, can you get seven glasses? Dad's not eating with us, is he?" asks TJ.

"No, he's stuck at work again," says Mrs. Walker. She points me to a cabinet next to the sink.

I've only seen Mr. Walker occasionally when we were playing outside and he got home from work on time.

"Why is he always stuck at work?" asks Rose, who's lounging at the table, flipping through a magazine.

"It's a new job," says Mrs. Walker. "That's how it is."

"It stinks," says TJ.

"It's fine," says Mrs. Walker. "We all need to make adjustments. It's important to be adaptable, and even if you're forced into it, change can be a good thing." She looks at Reggie, then adds, "Why doesn't everybody wash up? You girls use the bathroom downstairs. Boys upstairs. I'll finish the salad, and then we'll be ready to eat."

Reggie shuffles after TJ. I follow Chloe, Rose, and Daisy.

"Guests first," says Daisy.

I go into the bathroom and close the door. When I stare into the mirror, I almost don't recognize myself. I'm flushed from the excitement of the afternoon and the heat of the kitchen, and my face is framed by curly tendrils that have escaped from my ponytail. I look better than usual, I think, with the bathroom's warm yellow walls reflected in the mirror.

"Violet, c'mon," shouts Chloe from outside the door.

"Shh," I hear Daisy hiss.

"No, it's okay," I say, drying my hands on the thick white towel. "I'll be right out."

After Daisy, Rose, and Chloe crowd into the bathroom to wash their hands, the four of us file into the kitchen. At each table setting, Mrs. Walker has dished out a neat serving of lasagna and salad.

"You can sit next to me," says Chloe.

TJ rolls his eyes sympathetically at me from across the table as I position myself in the chair between Chloe and Reggie.

"Should we have a toast?" asks Mrs. Walker, raising her water glass. "To our new home. And to making new friends."

I hold my glass up, but I don't want to clink to Mrs. Walker's toast. It seems wrong to celebrate my own good luck. I put down my glass and bite into a forkful of steaming hot lasagna, gooey with cheese.

"So?" Mrs. Walker says. "Is everybody ready for school next week?"

"Really, Mom?" says TJ.

"We can't just pretend that the summer isn't ending," she says to TJ. "What about you, Violet? You must be looking forward to seeing your school friends, at least."

"Yeah, that will be good," I say. I'm not sure how it will be to see Katie.

"I bet I get homework on the first day," says TJ, shoveling lasagna into his mouth.

"I love homework," says Chloe. Even though she's only seven, she looks almost the same size at everyone else at the table because of her booster seat.

"You only like it because you barely got any last year," complains Rose.

"Did too. I'll probably get even more in second grade. Won't I get homework at Meadow Pond, Violet?" Chloe asks.

I think back to second grade. I remember recess and comfy chairs where we were allowed to read and a class turtle named Slowpoke.

"I guess you'll get a little," I say.

"See? Violet says I'll get homework in second grade."

"That's not exactly what she said," says Rose.

"Yes, it is."

"She said a little," says Reggie quietly.

"You can't even go to school by yourself, Reggie," Chloe snaps in return. "Mom, are you taking him the first day?"

"Chloe," warns Mrs. Walker.

"At the end of last year, she had to take him to school," Chloe says to me, as though she is doing Reggie a big service by explaining this. "Kids were so mean to him on the bus that he cried."

"I am not taking Reggie to school," says Mrs. Walker, serving herself more salad.

"Now you'll have to go on the bus like everyone else," Chloe says to Reggie.

"Chloe, just shut up," says Daisy under her breath.

"Mom! Did you hear her?" asks Chloe.

"I think that being quiet right now is not a bad idea."

"What I said was true," Chloe says.

"It's *true* that you have a big mouth," says TJ.

"That's enough," says Mrs. Walker, putting her fork down on her plate. "You guys know I don't like this kind of fighting." She looks out the kitchen window into the backyard. "It seems like the rain has stopped. When you finish eating, you can go outside before Violet has to go home. Chloe, you'll stay here and help me, and we'll have a talk."

"But our team won," whines Chloe. "They should do the dishes!"

"I don't mind doing the dishes," I say. It actually sounds kind of fun to do the dishes with Reggie and TJ. TJ can wash, I can dry, and Reggie can put them away.

"That's okay. I'd like to speak with Chloe alone," says Mrs. Walker.

"Let's go! We can try out that new Frisbee," says Rose as she dumps her plate into the sink.

"I kind of stink at Frisbee," I say.

"It's all right," says Reggie. "I doubt I'll be good either." Reggie always seems to be looking out for me; he notices whenever I'm getting that awkward or embarrassed feeling. And for someone who doesn't talk much, he knows how to say just the right thing, at least when it comes to me. I wonder if I would like the Walkers so much if Reggie wasn't there to come to my rescue.

"It doesn't matter," says TJ. "I'll give you guys some pointers."

"What about me?" asks Chloe with her hands on her hips.

"*You* are staying to help Mom," TJ says as we all head outside.

●●●●●●●●●●●

When I get back from the Walkers', my mother's in her bedroom, sitting on the bed with her legs stretched out and a stack of folders at her feet. On the top of the pile is a paper that says "Instructions for Your EpiPen."

I sit down on my father's side of the bed.

"Did you have fun over there?" my mother asks. Instead of waiting for me to answer, she says, "Finally, a product I don't need to research. Who knew that having an allergy would ever come in handy? Maybe I can even get a discount on my next prescription," she adds with a laugh. "So, it was fun?"

"Really fun," I say.

"And..."

She's looking at me like I'm one of those pinned-down bugs in the little dishes that we looked at in science last year.

"What did you do?" she asks.

"I don't know. We had dinner."

"How was the lasagna? Did Mrs. Walker make it herself?"

When I nod, my mother looks bothered.

"I think you'd like her," I say, even though I don't mean it.

"I'm not sure she's my type."

"How do you know?"

"I don't for sure. But no matter what, it doesn't mean that you can't be friends with the kids. What else did you do?"

"Nothing," I say.

I don't want to tell her that the best part of the day was at the end when Rose, Daisy, TJ, Reggie, and I were playing Frisbee. TJ tried to help me throw in a straight line, but no matter where I aimed, the Frisbee seemed to go anywhere else. Once, I let go at the wrong time and the Frisbee got stuck on a low branch in the oak tree. TJ told Reggie he could climb up to get it but instructed the rest of us not to mention this incident to anyone, particularly big-mouthed Chloe. The four of us watched while Reggie quickly inched up the tree like an expert and rescued the Frisbee.

As soon as he came down, he pointed at a small hole in the lawn and asked me, "Did you see that?"

"I didn't see anything," I said.

"I just saw a snake go in there."

"Dad's not going to be happy with a snake digging up the grass," TJ said.

"Snakes don't usually make the holes themselves," said Reggie. "Usually it's just chipmunks or mice that make the holes. The snakes only use them."

"Whatever," TJ said. "Dad is not going to be pleased. C'mon, Reggie, let's play." He grabbed the Frisbee out of Reggie's hand and motioned the two of us back to our spots. Rose and Daisy were already bored of Frisbee and had started practicing their soccer drills.

Reggie, TJ, and I spent the rest of the time throwing the Frisbee back and forth while we talked about nothing and everything—like questions adults ask us that we find annoying. TJ's top favorite annoying question was "What do you want to do when you grow up?" Reggie thought that the worst question was "What's your favorite subject in school?" because, duh, it's school, and it stinks to have to pretend that you have a favorite subject.

My least favorite question comes up when someone finds out you like to do something and then proceeds to ask you why you like to do it. Even though I like to draw, I hate when anyone wants to talk about it. I really don't want to tell them that I like drawing because it's just the right amount of productive and comforting. That seems like a strange and slightly pathetic thing to say. And if I tell them that, then the next time I pick up a pencil in front of them, there's a good chance they're going to think I'm doing it because I need to be comforted.

The three of us agreed that explaining things you like spoils them. That's why I don't want to tell my mother about my day—it would definitely ruin it.

 Five

ON Labor Day weekend, my father doesn't need to fly to Atlanta until Tuesday, so I spend the night at his apartment on Sunday instead of Saturday. At the diner that night, I'm telling him about the Walkers when the waitress, Laurie, interrupts. "What's everyone having?"

My father always wants Laurie to be our waitress because she brings me an extra basket of the breadsticks I love and remembers that my father likes to have his drink with his meal and not before it, and that he always gets a cup of decaffeinated coffee after he eats.

"Hmm, I think I'll have the special," says my father, closing the menu as if he were actually considering ordering something else.

After dinner and dessert, we return to my dad's apartment, and I watch a movie alone because he has work to do. To make it up to me, on Monday afternoon he takes me to the office supply store, my most favorite place in the world. I love browsing through the notebooks and planners—all of those things that make you feel like you could design the perfect life. My dad buys me a planner and some binders and gel pens for school. He even gets me some new drawing supplies: a fancy pad and pastel crayons—ones you can use to make edges look soft and pretty just by smudging them.

After he drives me back home, I gather up my purchases and he gets my overnight bag out of the trunk.

"So, everything's going okay here?" my father asks as we walk up to the front door. Since he only sees me on the weekends, he likes to stretch out the amount of time we have together as long as possible. We usually end up sitting on the front porch so that he can ask me questions he's usually already asked before. It seems like he really hates to leave, and I sometimes wonder if he misses living here.

My mother hears us talking outside and opens the door.

"Hey, Sam. Do you want to come in?"

"No, that's all right. Some other time. I've got work to get back to," he says.

"Okay, then," she says, closing the door.

He turns to me and asks, "Your mother's been doing all right?"

"She's fine."

"Good, good. And you? Not too nervous about Wednesday? It's a big change going to middle school."

Even though I usually have jitters in the weeks before

school starts, I've been so busy with the Walkers I've barely thought about it.

"I think I'm okay."

"I guess there's nothing for me to worry about, then. I'm really glad," he says, giving me a kiss on the cheek.

●●●●●●●●●●●●

After my father leaves, I dump my overnight bag in the hallway, quickly show my mom the new stuff he got me, and then start across Goldie's path to the Walkers' house. I can see that Mr. Walker is outside, watering a tree that he planted at the top of the driveway.

I'm halfway across the path when I notice Reggie. Even though he's crouching down, Reggie's pretty tall, so I can still see him in the middle of the overgrown weeds and trees that make up the strip between our houses.

"What are you doing?" I ask.

He puts his finger on his mouth to shush me.

"It's a yellow warbler," he whispers, pointing at a low branch. The bird is small and bright yellow with brown streaks on its belly. It's hopping back and forth between trees, whistling. When I approach, it flies up to a higher branch.

"Do you hear that? They're really easy to identify because of their sound. The bird books all say it sounds like *Sweet, sweet, I'm so sweet.*"

He sits down in the weeds and closes his eyes tightly to concentrate.

"*Sweet, sweet, I'm so sweet.* I keep trying, but I just don't hear it that way. Anyway, they do sound distinctive—you can definitely tell they're warblers," Reggie says.

I crouch down to join him.

"Hey, be careful where you sit. When Chloe was out here earlier, we saw a snake. I think it's that same one from the yard. It's just a garter, but it's pretty big."

"Ooo-kay," I say, standing up.

"Don't worry. I bet Chloe scared it away. She freaked out and started screaming at the top of her lungs before she ran back inside. She's probably in the kitchen with our mother and Rose and Daisy talking about the first day of school. You should probably go in anyway. My mother said she wants to talk to you, too."

"I guess," I say. "If she really wants to talk to me."

"She does," he says. "You're part of the plan."

I like being part of the plan. I smile at him and then at Mr. Walker, who waves at me as I head to the back door.

Mrs. Walker opens the door holding her legal pad. "I'm so glad you're here, Violet," she announces. "Have a seat."

I sit down next to Daisy at the kitchen table.

"I'm just going over the school bus schedule," Mrs. Walker says, examining her list. "TJ needs to be at the corner at seven-thirty, Reggie at eight, and the girls at eight-thirty. I am wondering if you can ride the bus with Reggie."

"Sure," I say.

"That's wonderful. Girls, we need to go through everyone's backpack tonight and make sure the school supplies are all straightened out in case I need to make another run to the store tomorrow," Mrs. Walker says, putting her legal pad to the side. "Do you know what you're going to wear the first day?"

"I do," says Chloe. "I'm going to wear my red gauzy dress with sandals and my rainbow hairband."

"That red dress is nice for parties, but not for your first day of school," says Mrs. Walker.

"You told me I could wear something I like," whines Chloe.

"Something you like that works for school."

"Didn't you say you wanted to wear your blue skirt?" asks Daisy. "It's so pretty. And that new flowered shirt?"

"I don't know," says Chloe.

She never voluntarily agrees to anyone's suggestions, so it's fun to watch Daisy feed Chloe ideas that make Chloe think that she came up with them herself. Pure genius, if you ask me.

"You should show that skirt to Violet and see what she thinks," says Rose. "She used to go to Meadow Pond."

"Yes, Violet would know what's appropriate," agrees Mrs. Walker.

"What does *appropriate* mean?" asks Chloe.

"It means doing the right thing for the particular occasion."

"Oh, okay. Violet, let's go," Chloe says, pulling on my arm.

As she drags me out the door, I look back at Rose, who smirks because she's used me as bait so that she's not the one to be dragged. When Chloe gets me into her room, we go straight to her small but organized closet. One side has dresses neatly hanging with a bin at the bottom for shoes. The other side has skirts and jackets and shirts. Chloe grabs a hanger with a blue pleated skirt and holds it in front of her.

"That one would be absolutely perfect," I say. Although I am pouring on the enthusiasm, I have to admit that the skirt is really pretty.

"Wait! I haven't shown you the shirt that would go with it." Chloe reaches up and pulls a white shirt with little yellow flowers out of the closet.

"Would this be appropriate for Meadow Pond?" she asks.

"Definitely."

Chloe's already got more style than I ever will. Right now, she's got on a purple T-shirt that's been artfully cut at the bottom, fancy white shorts, and colorful long socks. She's fastened her ponytail neatly with a ribbon that matches her shirt. I can tell just by looking at her that it won't take long for Chloe to rule Meadow Pond. She will be one of those girls everyone else tries to imitate.

"What are you going to wear the first day?" Chloe asks.

"I'm not sure," I say, even though I have a possibility in mind. I had picked out a blue shirt with three little buttons down the front that I could wear with my best shorts, the ones I got from my mother's old client Home Away from Home Camp Wear.

For that account, my mother had to write a description of each piece of camp clothing, and I got to keep the samples. Even though my mother doesn't care about clothes herself, she's really good at coming up with catchy little phrases that make you want to buy stuff. Like what she wrote about my shorts: "A cut above average, these denim hipsters will be the ones you put on again and again." And she was right.

"Tell me," Chloe insists. "What are you wearing?"

"Probably shorts and a polo shirt," I say.

"Older kids wear shorts, right?" she says. "That's what Rose and Daisy are doing, too."

"I guess."

"I'm glad I'm not older," says Chloe. "I like skirts. They're more special."

The fact that Chloe says whatever comes into her head is weirdly entertaining. I wonder if that's how all little kids are—though I don't ever remember being like that myself.

"You're right," I admit. "I think when you get older, you want to be more comfortable."

"When I'm older, I won't care about being comfortable," Chloe declares.

"You might."

"Nope," she says. "I'll want to look good."

"I'm sure you will," I say, nodding.

"Chloe, are you trying on your entire closet?" Rose yells from the kitchen. "Violet doesn't need the whole fashion show."

"She likes it," insists Chloe as she slams the closet door shut.

"But other people might want to talk to her," shouts Rose, and I laugh.

"Are you making fun of me?" Chloe asks.

"No," I say. "I wouldn't make fun of you."

"Rose and TJ do. They think I don't understand, but I always do."

"They're probably just kidding around," I say as I follow her out. "Isn't that what brothers and sisters do?"

"I guess," she says. "But how do you know? You don't have any brothers and sisters."

"I can imagine."

"That's not the same," Chloe says, skipping ahead of me.

Six

"DO you want me to go to the bus stop with you this morning?" my mother asks on Wednesday as she washes out our cereal bowls.

I can't believe she's asking. Even on first days, I've been walking to the corner by myself for at least two years.

"Or I could drive you and drop you off," she offers. "I'm sure middle schoolers don't want their parents hanging around at the bus stop anyway."

Any other time, I would have been thrilled to have her drive me. But this year, I have it all planned out. Mrs. Walker asked if I could meet her and Reggie at their house at 7:40, and then the three of us will walk the five minutes to the corner. Mrs. Walker wants to wait with us until the bus comes at 8:00.

TJ will already be gone, and Rose and Daisy will help Chloe get ready while we're at the bus stop. They'll wait for

Mrs. Walker to come back before they all head down to the bus stop together.

"That's okay," I say to my mother. "I'm going to walk with Reggie. He's the one in my grade. I already talked to him about it yesterday."

I should tell her that Mrs. Walker is going to the bus stop with us, too, but I don't.

"Okay, then," she says, kissing me on the cheek. "Have fun." She grabs me and squeezes, resting her head on top of mine for a second.

"I will," I say as I squeeze her back.

After I leave, I turn around and see her waving through the living room window. I wave back and then jog-run toward the Walkers' back door.

I tap softly, but Mrs. Walker hears me right away. She must have been standing right near the mudroom door.

"C'mon in, Violet," she says, leading me into the kitchen. It's bright and cozy and smells like maple syrup and bacon. There are dishes piled in the sink; even though the kids are leaving at different times, they must have all eaten together. Yesterday Chloe told me that they always have pancakes on the first day of school. I try not to feel hurt that the Walkers didn't ask me over for breakfast. Why would they? Mrs. Walker probably assumes that my mother and I have our own special first-day of school tradition.

"Reggie went to get his backpack, and then we can leave. I don't want you guys to miss the bus on your first day." Mrs.

Walker is wearing a white shirt and jeans and brown clogs. Her hair is pulled back into a bun on the top of her head, and her lips shimmer with pale pink lipstick. "I am so glad that you'll be on the bus with Reggie," she whispers to me. "We moved so late, there wasn't an orientation for him to attend. He's going to really appreciate having someone who knows their way around."

"Sure," I say, hoping she's not overestimating my abilities. Even though I have the benefit of last spring's orientation tour, I don't remember much more than which building our classes will be in and where the bathrooms are.

"Lunch will probably be the hardest part for him," Mrs. Walker adds. "It's always tough to be the new kid, and sometimes it just takes Reggie a little longer to make friends. He doesn't want you to think that you *have* to sit with him, but it's nice that he'll know that you're there somewhere."

"That's okay," I say. "I could definitely sit with him."

"Are you sure?" she asks.

I nod vigorously although I'm already worrying. I wonder if Mrs. Walker is also overestimating my ability to help Reggie feel at ease. It's not like I ever walk into the cafeteria with great confidence myself. And it is going to be a new year. *And* it's middle school with a new cafeteria. Plus I haven't seen Katie all summer. Anything can happen.

"You're so sweet. I feel so much better knowing he's not alone."

She smiles at me, and I feel myself blushing.

"C'mon, Reggie," Mrs. Walker shouts toward the stairs. "Violet's waiting."

When Reggie comes into the kitchen, his hair is still wet and he's carrying a blue backpack.

"It's going to be great. A whole new start. Daisy, make sure you and Rose and Chloe are ready to go when I get back!" Mrs. Walker yells as we leave.

Reggie and I walk next to each other behind Mrs. Walker, who keeps a brisk pace as she leads us to the bus stop. From about halfway down the street, I can already see clusters of kids and someone's parent standing at the corner.

I feel like a different person coming to the bus stop with the Walkers. If I came by myself, I don't think anyone would notice me, but right now people are obviously watching the three of us approach them.

Owen Simon is standing next to his mother. When we reach the corner, Mrs. Walker goes right up to Owen's mother and holds out her hand.

"I'm Sabrina Walker. We moved into the neighborhood a few weeks ago."

"Amanda Simon."

"So nice to meet you. This is my son Reggie. And you must know Violet—who lives next door to us," adds Mrs. Walker, gesturing at me.

"Yes, of course."

Despite the words coming out of her mouth, Mrs. Simon doesn't look sure that she knows me, even though I have been going to school with Owen since we were little kids.

"Have you lived in the neighborhood a long time?" Mrs. Walker asks Mrs. Simon.

Mrs. Simon points behind her. "We've been in this house for about eleven years. We moved in when my older son was starting kindergarten."

"You have one on the earlier high school bus? My other son, TJ, is on that bus. They want nothing to do with you at this point, right?"

"Jack barely says goodbye when he leaves," Mrs. Simon agrees with a laugh.

I can tell that Mrs. Simon already likes Mrs. Walker.

"Owen, did you say hello to our new neighbors?" asks Mrs. Simon, who suddenly seems to remember why she's at the bus stop.

"Hey," says Owen. Even though his mother is by his side, he's somehow able to take this potentially popularity-crushing detail in stride. I guess it's because Owen has been cool since the third grade, when coolness became a thing. He usually spends most of his time at the bus stop talking about the Yankees and swinging an imaginary bat in the air. It occurs to me that Reggie might dump me for him, but maybe he's not in love with baseball the way Owen is.

"Owen, meet...I'm sorry, what did you say your name was?" Mrs. Simon asks Reggie.

Reggie whispers his name.

"I don't think Mrs. Simon can hear you," says Mrs. Walker. She doesn't say it in a mean way, but Reggie still looks annoyed as he repeats his name for Owen.

"And you said you know Violet?" Mrs. Walker asks Mrs. Simon.

"I met your parents some years ago," Mrs. Simon says to me as if she's just figuring it out now. "Sam and—and—Eva, right?"

I nod.

My mother's name sounds so old-fashioned and nasally when Mrs. Simon says it. And something about the way Mrs. Simon emphasizes my mother's name makes me think that she knew it all along, and that her hesitation before saying it means something else. Maybe Mrs. Simon knows that my father has moved out and that my parents are no longer officially Sam-and-Eva.

"Mrs. Walker also has a son in high school," Mrs. Simon says to Owen, as though he hadn't been standing right here for the whole conversation. "Didn't Jack say that he met someone from the neighborhood at the baseball field this weekend?"

"Yeah, said he has a good arm," says Owen.

"That must be TJ. Though Reggie does, too," says Mrs. Walker, smiling encouragingly at Reggie.

It seems like she hopes he's going to say something about baseball, but instead he stares at his feet.

"I think TJ mentioned your son Jack to me, too," Mrs. Walker adds. "It's so nice they have a common interest."

"Makes such a difference," says Mrs. Simon.

I can already picture Mrs. Simon and Mrs. Walker putting

together the annual baseball-team fundraiser. Maybe it will be one of those potluck dinner things with an auction; maybe Mrs. Walker will make her lasagna again.

The bus turns onto the street and kids start to peel off from their groups and form a crooked line. When the bus pulls up to the stop, Mrs. Simon checks her watch. "Eight o'clock on the dot. I guess the kids got Irene as their bus driver this year. She's a stickler for the schedule." She looks around to say goodbye to Owen, but he's already moved away from us to the back of the line. It's uncool to be one of the first ones on the bus.

"Have a good day," says Mrs. Walker to Reggie. "Violet will keep a lookout for you. Right?" She puts her arms loosely around both of us. I lean into the hug and get a whiff of her perfume. She smells like soap and citrus and flowers.

"Sure I will. Of course."

Reggie looks miserable. I wonder if he's hoping that his mother might give him a break and let him skip the first day of school and try again tomorrow. We board the bus as she waves cheerfully to us.

●●●●●●●●●●●●

I may not be as nervous as Reggie about the first day of school, but I'm still nervous. At least I know that I'll have Katie in my traveling class, which means that we have all of our classes together. It's what they do for seventh graders in middle school.

Katie and Missy both went to a sporty sleepaway camp in

Maine where campers spend every single day playing soccer and tennis and learning to sail and do archery. Katie and I promised to write each other all the time, but that didn't end up happening. She did write me a long letter right after she got there describing what she and Missy were doing together, which was kind of hard to read about, and then I wrote her a long letter back and that was it.

Texting or calling would have been so much easier, but there was a no-technology rule at the camp. Then we were going to see each other right after Katie got back, but she ended up leaving for a family vacation. We did text each other when we got our class assignments, and we were both really excited when we figured out that we were in the same traveling class. Katie was upset that Missy ended up in a different one, and even though I pretended to commiserate with her, I was relieved.

Having one good friend in your traveling class is all you need because you can figure things out together. And that's going to be important because Franklin Middle School is nothing like Meadow Pond Elementary. For one thing, it's so big that they had three orientations last spring—one for each of the elementary schools that feed into it.

The bus bumps its way along a winding web of roads, picking up about twenty kids. Reggie gave me the window seat, and he spends most of the ride with his head turned away from me, gazing across the aisle and out the other window. There's not much to look at, but the neighborhoods are pretty. The morning light sets off the tree-lined streets, and all the lawns are lush and green from summer-afternoon rain showers. Reggie and I don't really talk, but it doesn't feel weird or awkward. I think I'm more comfortable with Reggie than I would be with anyone else on the bus, including the people I've gone to school with my whole life.

The bus pulls into the school driveway, and we get off. The principal and some of the teachers cheerfully welcome everyone as we funnel through the double doors. People are pushing and yelling with excitement, and in the growing crowd, Reggie looks pale and small.

All of the seventh grade classes are in Building B. One of the teachers is shouting, "B-100 to B-110 hallway to the left. B-111 to B-120 hallway to the right." She waves her arms as though she were directing a plane on a runway.

"That way," I yell so that Reggie can hear me over the crowd.

He turns right, and I follow him, ignoring the kid who's stepping on my heels from behind as I check the room numbers.

"Here's yours," I say. "And there's mine next door. You going to be okay?"

"Sure," Reggie says, although he doesn't look confident.

I don't prod him any more, but I also think back to Chloe's stories and the promise I made to Mrs. Walker this morning. I remember Mrs. Walker's loose embrace at the bus stop.

"Do you want to come find me in the cafeteria during lunch?" I ask.

"I'm fine," he says.

"Just look for me," I insist. "I'll be there."

Reggie nods in my direction before he shuffles through the door. I see Reggie's homeroom teacher, Mrs. Schein. She was one of the leaders at last year's orientation program. She has short grayish hair, and on orientation night she wore a thick, homemade-looking sweater and a colorful pin in the shape of an owl. From the way she dresses, you would think she's warm and fuzzy, like a kind grandmother, but she's not. Everybody says she calls people by their last names, as in, "Miss Crane, I see you haven't done your homework. Would you like to tell the class why you were unable to complete it?" When I found out that Reggie had Mrs. Schein, I didn't have the courage to tell him or Mrs. Walker about her reputation.

I head into my homeroom. Katie waves wildly at me from her seat in the middle of the room. "Yay! Sit here, Violet," she says, pointing to the chair next to her. Rachel Fieldston, a girl we sometimes ate lunch with at Meadow Pond, is already sitting on Katie's other side.

Ms. Santorini, our homeroom teacher, is perched on the edge of her desk at the side of the room watching everyone file in. She has speakers playing classical music, and her feet swing back and forth in time as she waits. The music helps calm the butterflies in my stomach.

"If you can hear me, clap once," Ms. Santorini says, and then she stops the music and hops off her desk. The talking continues. "If you can hear me, clap twice."

It's embarrassing that she still has to use this technique with us in middle school, but it works and we clap twice. The room goes silent as we size one another up. These are the people we're going to be stuck with for the whole year—the ones we'll have to work with on group projects and in science labs.

"Welcome to seventh grade, boys and girls," Ms. Santorini says as she writes her name carefully on the whiteboard. "Not only will I be your homeroom teacher this year, but I am also your social studies teacher. You will be seeing me a lot! Let's use this time before you head to math to get ourselves organized."

Katie makes a face at me when she hears the word *math*. She hates math. Last year our teacher would randomly call on kids to share answers from their homework on the board at the front of the room, and Katie would almost always get her problem wrong. Then the teacher would ask her to go through the problem step by step so she could see where she made her mistake. You would think that teachers would get what a bad idea that is. If you didn't understand the problem when you were at home by yourself, how could it help to make you try and figure it out while you're standing in front of everyone else in the class? I'm always amazed by how some adults are just not that smart when it comes to understanding kids.

After taking roll and going through other first-day stuff, Ms. Santorini says, "I will be giving out locker assignments later, but for now gather up what you will need this morning. Fourth period, you will return to this room for social studies. Lunch will be fifth period, so those of you who brought a lunch may leave it on the shelf in the back of the room."

The bell rings, and Ms. Santorini sends us on our way.

Math is uneventful. The teacher introduces the thrill that will be algebra and goes through the always-boring list of "classroom expectations." When the bell rings we head down the hallway to the gymnasium.

After that is English, in which Mr. Hardy has us play "get to know one another" bingo and tells us that we're supposed to play with someone new to us. A girl behind Rachel quickly asks her to be her partner for the game. Katie laughs and says since she and I didn't see each other during the summer, we each would qualify as a "someone new."

Of course, I already know a lot about Katie. We met in third grade when her family moved to town. We sat at the same table, and she says I taught her how to draw an elephant, though I don't remember knowing how to draw an elephant myself back then. I know that Katie always colors her elephants and everything else aqua blue because she loves the ocean and that her favorite sandwich is turkey and cheddar with mustard, no mayo, because mayo is the most disgusting creation on earth. She knows that my favorite is avocado and tomato but that I don't eat it that often because avocado upsets my stomach.

By the time bingo is over, we've fallen back into the natural rhythm of our friendship. We link arms as we go to social studies, which is also uneventful because after Ms. Santorini explains that we will be focusing on the U.S. government and takes a poll about how familiar people are with current events, a kid named Benjamin wants to tell the class absolutely everything that he knows about what is going on in the world.

And then it's finally lunchtime. Katie, Rachel, and I go together. Rachel is small with silky brown hair and walks with her head erect and her toes pointed out. At the end of each school day last year, she changed into a black leotard and pink tights cut off at the ankles so she'd be ready for her dance class at a professional ballet school. I always wondered if I wore that outfit and put my hair in a bun with a net like she did if I would miraculously become graceful. As we walk out, I stand up a little straighter and point my toes out like Rachel does.

We get to the cafeteria and it smells fishy—they must be serving fish sticks today.

"Let's grab that table in the corner," says Katie, pulling me by the arm so that I follow her. I should be happy, but I don't know what to do about Reggie. I turn around to see if I can spot him in the crowd.

"Okay, but..." I say. "It's just—I have to watch out for my neighbor."

"Who?" Katie asks.

"Remember, I told you about him during English. His family moved in next door to us. I said I'd look for him in the cafeteria. He's in Mrs. Schein's traveling class," I explain.

"Why do you have to?" Katie asks.

"I told him I would," I say.

"We have to take this table before someone else gets it," Katie says.

I follow her but turn around every few seconds to make sure that Reggie isn't looking for me. We sit down, and Katie and Rachel unpack their lunchboxes. Katie has a thermos, and Rachel has a salad in a big plastic tub. When Missy's class comes in, Missy spots us and grabs the last empty seat next to Katie. Missy has one of those bento-box lunches where every kind of food has its own compartment. I have a paper bag. My mother has packed me a turkey sandwich and apple slices that have already turned an unappealing shade of light brown.

"Ugh, I can't believe the summer is over," says Katie, wrenching the lid off her thermos and tearing open a package of oyster crackers.

"Yeah. Wasn't camp great?" asks Missy. "We had the best counselors!"

"It was so cool. You guys should have seen the show we were in at the end," Katie says to me and Rachel. "Our bunk won all the prizes."

"What kind of show?" asks Rachel. She dumps dressing into her salad tub and shakes it.

"Singing and dancing."

"What kind of dancing?" Rachel asks.

"Not ballet or anything, not like stuff you do," says Katie.

"I don't just do ballet. I do some modern, too. I was in a special program this summer, and we all got to be fairy nymphs and wear these crazy costumes."

"How was Lanford Day Camp?" Katie asks me before she carefully spoons some chicken soup into her mouth. Katie's soup smells so good. I've never even thought of bringing soup for lunch, although it would be pretty easy to do. I have to remember to ask my mother to get some at the grocery store the next time she goes.

"I mostly helped out with the little kids," I say.

"Bummer," says Missy. "The day camp I used to go to was lame."

"No, it was pretty fun," I say. "Anyway, after camp ended, I've mostly been hanging out with our new neighbors, the Walkers."

Missy shrugs. She's not impressed.

I scan the cafeteria again for Reggie, but there are so many people moving around that I can't see him. I get up from my seat, and then I spot him—standing like a statue in the cafeteria doorway.

"Reggie!" I shout across the room. A couple of people nearby turn to look, and everyone at my table seems annoyed.

"Geez," says Katie.

"Well, he looks lost," I say.

"How can he be lost? It's the cafeteria," says Missy.

Reggie must have heard me, because he starts to walk in

our direction. I can't be sure, though, because he doesn't try to make eye contact. Instead he stares at the floor ahead of him as if he were desperately trying to follow a trail through the woods. When he approaches us, there aren't any chairs left at our table, so he just stands there.

"Guys, this is Reggie," I say. My voice comes out louder than I mean it to be.

"There are no more seats," states Missy.

I turn to Reggie and say, "I'll get you one."

At the table next to us, Owen is sitting with his friend Jake, the Meadow Pond class clown, and there's one extra chair between them.

Instead of asking Owen for that chair, which seems impossibly embarrassing at the moment, I quickly skirt around them until I reach Ann and Beth's table. Ann and Beth are two serious girls I know from Meadow Pond who play the violin and cello, though I can never remember which one plays which.

"Are you using this?" I ask.

"Go ahead," says Ann.

I grab the chair and drag it behind me. I haven't reached our table yet, but the scraping sound makes Owen look up, and he notices Reggie standing there, caught between our table and his.

"Hey, bro, sit with us," says Owen.

"It's okay," says Reggie.

"C'mon, sit down."

Reggie looks at me for help. I don't say anything because I don't know what to say.

"All right," Reggie says. He doesn't look at me again and walks toward Owen's table.

Awkwardly, I stick the borrowed chair I'm clutching under our table and sit back down.

"This guy's brother is like a star pitcher," I hear Owen say to Jake. "My brother says he's going to transform the high school baseball team in the spring."

"Do you play?" Jake asks Reggie.

"Not really," says Reggie.

"A bunch of players on the middle school team graduated," says Owen. "We're going to need some new blood."

"Who says you're even making the team this year?" Jake asks Owen.

"My brother made the team in sixth grade, and I'm way better than he was," Owen replies. "Maybe Reggie is even better than his brother."

From our table, I watch Reggie from the corner of my eye. As he takes out a sandwich and starts to eat, Owen and Jake laugh and talk, but Reggie doesn't join the conversation. When he's finished with his sandwich, he begins to carefully peel an orange.

"Are you guys almost done? Let's go check out the fields," says Katie.

"Ready," says Rachel. She snaps together her salad container and puts it back in her polka-dotted lunch bag.

"Sounds good," I say. I've only finished half of my sandwich, but I'm not hungry anymore. I stick the other half in my paper bag, crumple the whole thing into a ball, and throw it into the trash.

Then I follow Katie, Rachel, and Missy out of the cafeteria.

As we leave, I try to meet Reggie's eyes, but he's concentrating on his orange, picking it apart section by section.

# Seven

OUR science teacher lets us out a few minutes early, so I am one of the first people on the afternoon bus home. I sit near the same spot I was in this morning so that Reggie can find me.

Reggie. When I think back to what happened at lunch, I feel sick to my stomach. I had planned to take care of Reggie—just like his mother had wanted—but somehow it hadn't happened. I can't stop thinking about what I should have done. Why didn't I make sure there was an empty seat for him at the table?

I remind myself that it wasn't all my fault. Reggie decided on his own to eat with those boys. He could have said no to Owen, but he didn't.

A bunch of loud boys pass by. They grab on to the tall seat backs and propel themselves forward, the rubber toes of their sneakers scraping the grooved black floor. The eighth-grade girls follow them, leaning on one another as they saunter along the aisle. They wear makeup—their eyelids sparkly and accentuated with dark pencil—as if they were going to a party instead of school.

I see Owen make his way toward the back. When Reggie appears behind him, it's obvious to me that Reggie could fit in with Owen and his friends, no problem. Mrs. Walker buys him all the right clothes: he's wearing the same uniform as all of the other cool boys—longish basketball shorts and a T-shirt that looks soft and fits him perfectly.

The only obvious difference between the popular boys on the bus and Reggie is the way he carries his backpack. Instead of letting it hang from one shoulder like they do, he's fastened his tightly, both straps squarely placed on his shoulders and the belt around the waist pulled hard. With his pack and his serious expression, he looks like he's ready for battle—or at least for a twenty-mile hike up a steep mountain.

I try to get Reggie's attention, but he doesn't give any sign of noticing me. He must have, though, because when he gets to where I'm sitting, he pivots and plunks down next to me. He doesn't take his backpack off, and the squarish bulk of it pushes him forward so he's sitting on the edge of the seat.

"Let me move my stuff over," I say.

I exhale and realize that I have been holding my breath since the minute I saw Reggie get on the bus. After what happened at lunch, I'm relieved that he has chosen to sit with me again.

"Thanks," he says, taking off his backpack. He pulls out his bird book and opens it on his lap.

"Isn't that a yellow warbler?" I ask, pointing to the photograph and thinking about how on Monday it had all felt different; there was still the possibility that everything would be magically perfect. *"Sweet, sweet, so sweet,"* I say.

"Yeah, right. Sweet. Or not," Reggie says.

"Was it bad?"

"What?"

"Lunch," I say. "You know I really wanted to—"

"I know," he interrupts. "It's fine."

"Were they nice? Owen and those guys?" I whisper it even though Owen and his friends can't possibly hear us.

"They're okay," he says.

"Maybe you'll be friends with them."

"I don't need friends."

I wonder for a moment if that includes me. Then Reggie surprises me.

"What about those girls you sit with? Are they your friends?"

"Of course," I quickly respond. "I mean, I guess so."

Katie's my friend, but I'm not sure Rachel and I have anything to say to each other when Katie's not there with us. Missy isn't particularly nice except to Katie and the boys she suddenly started noticing last year, although there doesn't seem to be much point in explaining that to Reggie.

"Is Mrs. Schein mean?" I ask instead. "I heard she kind of is, but I didn't know if I should tell you."

"She's okay," says Reggie.

It seems like he doesn't want to talk anymore, so I turn toward the window to give him some space. Reggie sighs loudly as he flips through his book. I wonder if he's been holding his breath, too.

The elementary school bus usually drops students home after the middle school bus, but today the elementary school has a shortened first day, so when we get off our bus, Chloe, Rose, Daisy, and Mrs. Walker are there waiting at the corner for us. Rose and Daisy are tapping a soccer ball back and forth to each other, and Chloe is sitting in the middle of a dusty patch of lawn by the side of the road with a stick in her hand. Year after year of kids waiting for the bus has worn down the grass and created a miniature sandbox by the side of the road on the edge of the Simons' lawn. When Chloe sees us, she gets up and throws the stick down in the dust.

"First day over! How'd it go?" Mrs. Walker asks Reggie. She's got that same tight smile she had on her face when Reggie got on the bus this morning. "Did you make some new friends?"

"It was fine," he says.

She smiles at him encouragingly and turns to me. "Thanks so much for looking out for him."

"Well, I..." I don't know what to say.

She looks at me with concern. "I thought you two would eat together. Did you not have the same lunch period after all?"

"Yeah, we did," says Reggie, picking up a small, speckled rock from the side of the road.

"It's just..." I start to say.

"We were with each other," Reggie says, throwing the rock down. "Everything was fine, Mom."

Reggie did sit at the table next to us, so it's kind of true. I don't know why he doesn't tell her that he sat at a table with Owen Simon. I'm sure Mrs. Walker would be happy that he'd made another friend.

"Oh, good. I baked some cookies. Can you come over, Violet?"

"We'll play soccer," says Rose.

"But TJ called Mom and said he needed to talk to his counselor about a class after school, so the teams won't be even," says Chloe, grabbing the soccer ball from Rose. "I'll play with you guys. It will be the three of us against Reggie and Violet."

Reggie has already started walking ahead of us, and his mother moves quickly to catch up to him. Chloe runs after them with the ball in her hand, and I stay back with Rose and Daisy. We spread out, three across the street like we own it. If a car comes through, we'll have to scatter, but no one suggests that we move to the side of the road.

Mrs. Walker doesn't even notice because she's busy talking to Reggie.

I picture what it would be like if my mother were here, too. She'd probably be nervous and unhappy, having to make conversation with everyone. I'd probably think about her the whole time and not get to have fun with Rose and Daisy.

"Daisy chain," says Rose, surveying the line the three of us make across the street.

"Flower power!" says Daisy.

"Best 'buds'!" I say. "All for one, one 'flor' all!"

Rose and Daisy laugh so hard that Mrs. Walker turns around to see what we're doing.

"I think your mom is 'stalking' us," I whisper.

Rose and Daisy laugh even harder.

"What are you girls up to?" Mrs. Walker asks. She says it with a smile, so I know she's not mad.

"Inside jokes, Mom," says Rose.

When we get to the Walkers', Mrs. Walker reminds me to let my mother know I'll be at their house.

"I'm starving! We'll meet you inside," Rose shouts at me as she sprints around back with Daisy following, braids flying.

I'm hanging out at the Walkers, I text my mom.

How was first day? she texts back.

Good. Tell u later, I write quickly as I head toward the house.

By the time I get to the backyard, everyone but Reggie is already inside. He's dumped his backpack on the ground beside his feet and is watching a crow eat on the rock. A couple of blue jays swoop in and take a stab at the crow.

"Wow! What was that?" I ask.

"My mother put table scraps out here again, and now they're fighting over them," says Reggie. "I told her not to do that, but she doesn't pay attention to me."

I nod, although I wonder whether, if the scraps weren't there, they'd be fighting over food somewhere else.

"I'd better go in," he says, picking up his bag. "My mother will probably send someone out to get me soon if I don't. She thinks I spend too much time by myself."

"But I'm here."

"Right," he says. "But you don't play baseball, and she really wants me to play baseball like TJ."

"I'm bad enough at soccer," I say, trying to make him laugh.

"You're not bad at soccer," he says. "You shouldn't put yourself down."

We head inside to the kitchen. There's a gallon of milk and a pyramid of thick peanut butter cookies on the table. Rose, Daisy, and Chloe are fighting for the biggest one, and Goldie is under the table sniffing around for scraps. Mrs. Walker stands at the sink cleaning up.

"Help yourself, Violet," says Mrs. Walker.

"They look delicious," I say, carefully taking a medium-sized cookie from the plate.

"Eat fast," says Rose. "Then we can all go outside and pretend it's still summer."

●●●●●●●●●●

Even though we're down a player and Rose and Daisy have the better ball skills, Reggie and I make a good team. He seems to know where I'll be before I even do, so when he passes the ball it always lands right in front of me.

Reggie kicks the ball from way down the field. It rises into the air and lands directly in the side of the goal, next to Chloe.

"No fair, Reggie! I didn't know you were trying to shoot it. We should use the announcement rule," says Chloe. "That's what we did in school today. You have to announce when you're taking a shot, or the other team gets the ball."

Mrs. Walker leaves to pick up TJ from school and by the time they get home, our soccer game is tied 1–1.

"TJ, if you want to play, we're playing with the *announcement* rule," says Chloe.

He rummages around in his backpack until he pulls out his baseball glove. "I can't play with you guys now. I need to work on my pitch. Which reminds me—Reggie, this guy I met at the pickup game last weekend lives down the street and says he has a brother named Owen who plays ball. Maybe you could practice with him and try out in the spring."

"Try out for what?" asks Reggie, his voice rising.

"For the Franklin baseball team."

"No thanks," says Reggie. He lets the soccer ball drop and gives it a big kick down to the other side of the lawn.

"Do you want to throw the ball with me now?"

"No *thanks*," Reggie insists.

"Don't you think Reggie should try out when he gets the chance, Violet?" TJ asks me.

"I don't know," I say.

"You might not always want to play soccer with Chloe after school," TJ says to Reggie.

"I'm not going to be able to play with you soon anyway, Reggie," says Chloe. "I'm going to be having a lot of play dates."

"My loss," says Reggie.

Reggie seems mad, but I don't understand why.

"You can be my catcher," says TJ.

"But we were playing soccer!" whines Chloe.

"You guys keep playing. Reggie and I can practice right over here."

"Why doesn't everybody just leave me alone?" Reggie says.

TJ turns away from Reggie and doesn't look back. While the rest of us play soccer, TJ throws a baseball into the net set up on the other side of the lawn. Sometimes a stray ball flies into our game and he comes to retrieve it. Other than that, he stays away from us.

Reggie and TJ's fight changes everyone's mood. We keep playing, but nobody has much energy. Even Chloe loses her killer instinct and sits down in the middle of the goal, plucking blades of grass from the lawn to use as whistles. (She had begged and begged until Reggie finally taught her how to do it.) Once Chloe sits down, Reggie walks away, wandering into the woods behind the house. Rose, Daisy, and I give up on the game and just kick the soccer ball back and forth until dinnertime.

 # Eight

"**HI,** Violet!" my mom calls out when she hears the front door shut.

I walk into her room. There's a big pile of folders where my father's pillow used to be, and from this angle it looks like a rectangular paper head.

"How did it go?" she asks.

"Fine."

"Good, good," she says as she thumbs through the folders. "Are you hungry?"

"I guess. What are we having?"

As part of their first-day-of-school tradition, the Walkers are having chicken and mashed potatoes with gravy for dinner. According to Chloe, chicken and mashed potatoes is everyone's favorite meal.

"Just sandwiches," she says. "I misplaced some papers earlier, and I spent most of the afternoon hunting for them.

I wanted to do something nice for dinner, but I just didn't get to it."

"Sandwiches are okay," I say. "I can make them."

"That would be a big help," says my mother, who's now furiously typing on her computer. "I should be done with this in about fifteen minutes."

In the kitchen I get out the sliced turkey and some leaves of slightly wilted lettuce. I put the sandwiches together on two plates but add carrot sticks and little piles of pickles. Then I pour two glasses of water and stare out the window at the backyard while I wait.

Since spending time with Reggie, I've started to pay more attention to what's going on outside. Once while we were waiting for TJ to find Reggie—he was in the woods with a pair of binoculars—Daisy told me that she thought Reggie would rather live with animals than with people. I can sort of understand it. Right now, a bunch of squirrels are chasing one another around in the backyard, having the time of their lives. They dash up and down the trees, playing what seems to be an energetic game of tag.

"Look at those squirrels," I say to my mother when she walks in the kitchen. "They're so cute."

"I never knew you were so interested in squirrels."

"Did you know that sometimes squirrels just pretend to bury food to trick their predators? That's what Reggie told me. And that their front teeth never stop growing."

"Hmm, I did not know that. Reggie sure knows a lot," she

says, sitting down next to me. "But enough about squirrels. I want to hear about your first day of middle school. How were your teachers?"

"My homeroom teacher, Ms. Santorini, seems nice. She also teaches social studies."

I look out the window again. The squirrels have stopped playing their game, and now two are sitting next to each other on the railing of the deck. They stare at me and my mother through the window with wide, unblinking eyes. As they watch, I get the feeling that they could be just like us, talking about how cute we are as we walk around the kitchen.

"What about your other teachers?" asks my mother.

"They seem fine. Ms. Kirk for math and Mr. Hardy for English. People say that he's been at the school forever. And I had art with Mrs. Moses. She seems great."

"I'll bet she's thrilled to have you in her class. Maybe she's even heard about you," says my mother.

"What do you mean?"

"Maybe she knows you won an art prize at Meadow Pond."

My mother doesn't understand how middle school actually works.

"I really don't think so. Anyway, I did meet some new kids," I say. "There's a girl named Samantha who's going to be my lab partner in science."

"Does she live in the neighborhood?" my mother asks, getting up to get herself more water.

"No one in my grade lives in the neighborhood except Reggie Walker and Owen Simon," I say.

"Oh, the Simons," she says, nodding. "They used to have a New Year's Day open house that everyone from the neighborhood was invited to."

"And you went?"

She nods. "They had two boys. As I remember, they were not very well-behaved."

"Owen's mother was with him at the bus stop this morning," I say, pouring myself a little dressing to dip the carrot sticks in.

"I wonder if she remembers."

"Remembers what?" I say.

"At one of the parties, Owen and his brother were throwing small red rubber balls at each other, and Owen hit you right in the face with one. You got so mad."

"Then what happened?" I ask.

"You picked up that ball and tried to hurl it straight at Owen's face."

"I did? Did I hit him?"

"Your aim wasn't great, so the ball landed in the dip bowl and the dip splashed all over Mrs. Simon."

I can't believe it. Perfect Mrs. Simon from the bus stop splattered with globs of dip.

"It was a mess," my mother says.

"But it was an accident," I say. "Right?"

"Sure. You were just reacting to being hit in the face. I had to pretend to scold you, but it was really kind of great." My mother lets out a big sigh and then finishes the last bite of her sandwich. "Delicious," she says. "Thank you."

Although my mother is ready to be done with the conversation, I can't stop thinking about this connection I have with Owen Simon, one that I don't remember at all.

"Was Mrs. Simon mad?" I ask.

"I'm sure she didn't like wearing that dip in front of her guests. Did she know who you were today?"

"I don't think she recognized me, but she seemed to remember you." I picture Mrs. Simon making that sour face this morning as she recalled my mother's name.

"She was always a little snooty," Mom says, getting up to rinse her plate and put it into the dishwasher.

Mrs. Simon does seem kind of snooty, but Mrs. Walker seems to like her.

"She didn't seem that bad," I say.

I don't really want to be defending Mrs. Simon, but I wonder how things might be different if she and my mother were friends. Like maybe I would be more comfortable around Owen. And if Owen and I were friends, then I might even be kind of popular. And then Missy would be nicer to me and I would feel better about Katie. It would probably have made everything easier.

 Nine

IT'S the second day of school, and the teachers are *still* explaining how we should organize ourselves and how we'll be graded. Except Ms. Santorini. She jumps right into a quick review of the three branches of government and how they work together. She reminds us of the role of the executive, judicial, and legislative branches, and then she has us form groups of three. Today the groups are supposed to come up with a new law for our school, and tomorrow we'll go through the process of trying to get the law passed.

Ms. Santorini allows us to pick our own group, which along with her habit of playing music during homeroom, is a reason she's sure to become everyone's favorite teacher. She says she trusts us to choose our partners but reminds us to take this privilege seriously.

Once we hear the news, Katie, Rachel, and I all squeal and move our desks together. Then Ms. Santorini comes around with worksheets and assigns each person in every group a different branch of government to represent.

I get the legislative branch.

"How about a law that says the cafeteria can't serve fish sticks anymore?" I ask, remembering the awful smell in the cafeteria yesterday.

"Hear! Hear! I agree," says Rachel. She's the judicial branch, so she bangs an imaginary gavel on the desk. "What do you think, Katie?"

"Whatever you guys want." She's busy folding and decorating a piece of paper to make a nameplate to prop up on her desk. It says President Katie Patterson and is surrounded by American flags. "Violet, can you help me draw the White House? Or, as I like to call it, *my* house!"

"I don't think we're really supposed to be doing that," I say.

"C'mon," says Katie. "Please, just a quick drawing."

I sketch a decent version of the White House with its triangular parapet above the columns of the portico, with the fountain in front. It looks pretty much how it's shown on the cover of the handout Ms. Santorini gave us.

"Ooo, I'm going to make a name tag, too," says Rachel. She gets out a piece of paper and writes *The Honorable Judge Rachel Fieldston* on top.

"Guys," I say. "We've got to do this."

"We *are* doing it," Katie says, continuing to color.

"Shouldn't we at least discuss the pros and cons?"

"Just write whatever you want," says Rachel. "I'm sure it will be fine." She picks up her imaginary gavel and flicks her wrist three times.

After I finish writing my proposal for outlawing fish and fish-like items, Ms. Santorini says it's time to get ready for lunch.

"What'd you write?" Rachel asks. "It's a group project, so we should all write the same thing."

Katie and Rachel copy down my paragraph and we get our lunches from the back of the room and get in line.

"Ugh. I hate the cafeteria. I can't wait until I'm in high school and we can go out for lunch," says Rachel. "My sister eats at the sushi place every day." Rachel's sister, also a dancer, is famous for starring in of all of the high school musicals.

"That would be awesome," says Katie. "I love sushi."

"Yeah, me too," I say, even though I don't really like sushi. I mean, I like the ginger and the wasabi, but not the fish part, and I'm pretty sure that liking the stuff that covers up the taste of the fish is not the same thing as liking sushi itself. Besides, I don't think my mother would be particularly happy about giving me money to eat out every day, especially since she never goes out to lunch herself.

When we get to the cafeteria, I quickly scan the room for Reggie. Owen and Jake are together at the same table they were at yesterday, but Reggie's not with them. As I wind through the tables behind Katie and Rachel, I see him sitting by himself. He's eating his sandwich and staring out the big window that opens onto a grassy circle in the front of school.

"There's Reggie," I say.

"Missy's already got us a table over there," says Katie.

"I should go sit with him."

"As president, I command you to stay with us," says Katie in her fake-serious executive-branch voice as she pulls my arm and sits down next to Missy.

"Hear! Hear!" says Rachel. She bangs her fist on the table, and they both crack up. Missy looks confused but laughs along.

"I'll be right back," I say.

I drop my lunch bag on the table and head toward Reggie. When I reach him I ask, "Do you want to sit with me? I'm over there with Katie, Rachel, and Missy."

"That's all right. I've got a good view here. There's a northern flicker in that tree over there. You don't see them that often around here."

"That's good, I guess. Are you sure you don't want to come with me?"

"I'm fine," he says. "We can just do something later at my house after school."

I know Reggie's making it easy for me again, and I'm grateful.

"It'll just be us," he adds. "Rose and Daisy signed up for after-school soccer, TJ has a pickup game, and Chloe's already got her first play date."

"Didn't take her long," I say.

"Nope," he says with a smile.

●●●●●●●●●●●●

After school, Reggie asks me what I want to do.

"Soccer drills?" I say.

"Nah," he says, kicking a rock in front of him.

"Some other game?"

"Nah," he says. Then he stops and leans in and whispers even though there's no one around us to hear. "Can you keep a secret?"

Can I keep a secret? Is the sky blue? Do chocolate chip cookies deserve their own food group? Will a golden retriever lick your face?

"I'm going to build a fort in a tree in the woods behind our house," he says.

"You are?" I say, tapping the rock that Reggie has kicked over to me.

"Yeah. I need my own private place to escape to, especially now that school has started. I wasn't going to tell anyone, but I guess I can tell you. We could even share it," he says tentatively. The look on his face reminds me of Goldie's—right before you throw a ball for her—serious and careful as she tries to anticipate which way you're going to throw.

"That sounds great."

"Don't you have to tell your mother you're here?" he says as we approach the back door.

"I'll text her, but she doesn't really pay much attention when she's working," I say.

"You're lucky," Reggie says.

He lets us into the house, and Goldie bounds in from the living room and jumps on Reggie, wild with excitement. Reggie kneels down and throws his arms around Goldie, who uses her tongue like a washcloth, cleaning his nose and his cheeks. Then she goes for one of his ears, licking it up and down.

"Stop, Goldie. That tickles!" he says, laughing so hard he has to sit down. Her tail wags furiously as if her plan has paid off, and she throws her whole self into his lap.

"You're too heavy for that. Here, girl," he says, patting the floor next to him.

Goldie sits, and Reggie rubs her head with long, gentle strokes until she settles down.

"Can you stay with her while I tell my mother we're going to walk her?" he asks, giving her one last pat on the head.

I sit down cross-legged next to Goldie. After she watches Reggie disappear, she uses me as a replacement, resting her heavy head in my lap. I stroke her a few times, and when I stop, she nudges me with her nose to remind me that she's still there.

"Such a smart girl," I say.

"She's the best," says Reggie as he comes back in. He picks up Goldie's leash from the basket in the mudroom and attaches it to her collar.

"I wish I were a dog," says Reggie. "Then I wouldn't have to go to school and do things I didn't want to do. Nobody would bother me. I could hang out all day sniffing around and digging holes."

"But there's stuff you'd miss," I say as we head out to the driveway.

If I were Reggie, I would definitely miss playing with his brother and his sisters and eating his mother's cookies and sitting on one of those comfy chairs in their living room and reading my book and about fifty other things, but it doesn't seem okay for me to point them out to him.

Reggie holds Goldie's leash tightly. He keeps it short so that she has to stay within a few feet of him as they walk.

"She runs after cars here. She never did before," he says. "If she decided to take off, I'm not sure I could stop her, and my family would never forgive me."

"Your family would understand."

"They would say they understand. But that doesn't mean anything."

After we take Goldie halfway down the block, Reggie turns her around and we start back. When we get to the Walkers' driveway, Reggie stops for a moment. He kneels down next to Goldie, cradles her head between his hands, and tenderly kisses her on the top of her nose.

I feel a little awkward standing there, witnessing this display of real love.

"Here you are, Goldie girl. Home, safe and sound," he says.

Ten

WHEN I leave for the bus stop the next morning, Reggie and his mother are already at the top of the driveway waiting for me. Mrs. Walker is not smiling, and Reggie seems mad.

"Nice to see you this morning, Violet," says Mrs. Walker, and then she immediately starts heading toward the corner as if she can't get there fast enough. As we walk, Reggie moves away so that I end up between him and his mother.

"Mrs. Simon says that some of the boys are getting together after school to play baseball, and I was just suggesting to Reggie that he might want to join them," Mrs. Walker says to me. "It might be a way to meet people, Reggie," she adds, looking over at him.

"I have other things I want to do after school," he responds.

"Dad and TJ both think you have real potential in baseball. And they know about these things."

I'm uncomfortable being in the middle of this discussion,

and take a small step back so they can walk next to each other.

"Why don't you ever listen to me?" Reggie asks.

"But TJ says he could practice with you," Mrs. Walker says.

"I don't want to practice," Reggie says.

He's so angry that it seems like people in whole other states would be able to see the storm clouds over his head. It's pretty embarrassing for me. So far, I've seen all of the Walker kids fight with one another at some point, but I've never seen a fight between Mrs. Walker and anyone.

"I don't want to," he repeats. "I'm not TJ."

"No one's asking you to be TJ," she says. She's so calm that you can tell that she thinks she's made the final, convincing point in the argument.

"Hey, Reg, did you see the game last night?" shouts Owen from the corner.

Reggie doesn't respond to Owen. Instead, he continues to glare at his mother—his fists clenched, his body rigid.

"Don't be rude. You're embarrassing me," Mrs. Walker whispers loudly.

"Fine," he barks.

I don't think Mrs. Walker should be embarrassed. Mrs. Simon isn't there, and I can't understand why she would care what Owen thinks of her.

"What game?" Reggie shouts at Owen. Even though his words don't give away his mood, his voice vibrates with anger.

"Go talk to him," says Mrs. Walker. "Start this year off on the right foot."

"Only if you leave," snaps Reggie.

As Reggie stomps toward Owen, Mrs. Walker turns around and walks right past me without saying anything, back toward her house. If she had looked at me at all, I'm sure I would have given her a small, sympathetic smile so that she'd know I understand she's just trying to help Reggie. But she never did.

"Yankees game, bro," I hear as Owen picks up the conversation with Reggie.

"Too busy," says Reggie.

"I'm never too busy. I'll fill you in," says Owen.

Reggie looks in my direction as if he wants me to rescue him, but I can't figure out how to do it. How am I going to rescue Reggie from Owen Simon, one of the most popular boys in school? Plus, I feel conflicted. I feel sorry for Reggie because he seems so mad, but I also know that Mrs. Walker probably only wants Reggie to fit in.

The bus appears and I get in line, but Reggie is still with Owen. Reggie follows him onto the line, so I guess I'm sitting alone. At least I was smart enough to keep a book in my bag, the way I always used to before the Walkers moved in. I sit down in the first empty seat a few rows back and take it out. Almost as soon as I do, Reggie is next to me.

"Can I sit here?" he asks.

I drag my backpack closer to the window to give him space.

"Bro, we're all sitting here," shouts Owen from the back of the bus.

"It's okay," Reggie says, moving his bag under my feet.

"Really? You're sitting there?" asks Owen.

Reggie doesn't respond.

"Your loss, bro," shouts Owen.

"Maybe you should sit with them," I say.

"No thanks."

"Your mother would want you to," I say, thinking about how anxious Mrs. Walker became when she thought Reggie wasn't going to try to talk to Owen.

"Yeah."

Even though I said it, I don't want him to agree with me.

"Go on and sit with him," I say.

"I told you. I don't want to."

"Really?"

"Really, *bro*," he says. "Unless you want me to. 'Cause it looks like you were going to read. What's that book about anyway?"

"It's hard to explain," I say, but Reggie nods encouragingly, so I try. "It's about this girl who gets bitten by a talking rat. She's kind of a quiet kid and has a hard time speaking up, but after the rat bites her, he talks for her and says all the stuff she'd really like to say."

"Wow, I could use one of those rats," he says.

"Me too."

"Owen, *bro*, I don't want to play baseball," he squeaks in

a rat voice before he switches back to his normal one. "I won-der if my mother would listen to me if I were a rat."

"Maybe," I squeak back.

"Does your mother bother you about who you hang out with?" he says seriously.

"Nah," I say.

"Or what you do?"

"Not really."

"Let's go to *your* house this afternoon, then," he says, then adds in his rat voice, "We can hang around in the kitchen and eat cheese."

"All right," I squeak. Then I say in my normal voice, "But let me go home first before you come over."

"Why?" asks Reggie.

"To make sure there aren't any rat traps out," I squeak again.

Throughout the day, I regret the whole cutesy rat talk that got me into this predicament. I do not want Reggie to come over to my house. He'll see that it isn't like anything like his. And my mother is sure to get nervous and say something embarrassing.

I think about all the ways I can keep Reggie from coming over: I can suddenly get the stomach flu, starting by making lit-tle moaning noises on the bus, then ramp it up so that by the end of the ride I'm threatening to vomit. Or I can go home and pretend that I'm ready for him to come over, but then run to his house early to intercept him by saying that *my mother* has a terrible stomach flu. I can do the same clutching and moaning but pretend to be her. It seems sad that no matter how creative I try to be, all of my excuses seem to involve throwing up.

When the dismissal bell finally rings, we pack up our bags for the day. I'm clinging to a glimmer of hope that Reggie might have forgotten about the whole idea.

"Hey," he says as he sits down next to me on the bus.

"Hey."

"Long day."

"Yep."

"Glad we rats have something to look forward to," he says, grinning at me.

"Right."

I turn my head toward the window and watch the houses go by. The noise on the bus is loud but joyous because it's Friday.

"I'm going to drop my stuff off and then I'll come over," Reggie says as soon as we get off the bus.

"All right." I forget to moan or clutch my stomach.

I climb up our front steps and do a quick comparison of my house and the Walkers'. We have an old black plastic welcome mat on our porch; the Walkers have a thick woven brown one. They have a flowerpot full of blooming plants in the corner; in that spot on our porch, there's a thin curved wall made of spiderwebs, complete with large spiders, the kind that appear to have settled in for the long haul.

I throw my bag down and grab a stick from the yard. As I stand poised in warrior mode about to cut through the web, I feel a pang of guilt and put the stick down. I can't destroy the web even though I remind myself that spiders are actually the lucky ones because they can make a new home for themselves whenever and wherever they want. Looking for another way to spruce things up, I pick up the black plastic mat and give it a good shake over the bushes until a cloud of dust envelops me.

My mother hears me open the front door and shouts from her room, "Hi, Violet."

"Hi," I yell back. "I have to tell you something."

"Come in here if you want to talk to me," she says.

"Reggie's coming over in a few minutes," I say, standing in her doorway.

"He is? You should have given me some warning. Do we even have any snacks to serve him?"

"It's okay. I'll find something."

"I guess you could make him a sandwich, or is he used to something special?" she asks.

I shake my head at her.

Out of everyone I know, Reggie doesn't ask for anything special from the people around him.

I hear a tap at the door. The next knock is louder, but short and quick.

I leave my mother there and run to the door. When I open it, Reggie has one foot on the top step and the other foot on the step below it, like he decided I wasn't going to answer and is heading home.

"Come in," I say, although the way I'm standing blocks the doorway. My throat feels tight and my hands are clammy. I wonder if this is what happens to my mother when she gets nervous.

"If it's okay," he says.

"I told my mom you were coming."

"That makes one of us. I just left," Reggie confesses.

"Why didn't you tell your mom you were coming here?"

"She wanted me to go play ball with Owen, so she might as well believe that's where I am. Anyway, I guess I really shouldn't have invited myself over," he says, and then steps inside. "I could tell you really didn't want me to come, but I needed to get away."

"From what?" I say, thinking that if I lived at the Walkers', I would never want to be anywhere else.

"From *them*. They always think I don't know how to act when they're not telling me what to do."

Before I can think of anything to say, my mother is suddenly standing right next to us.

"You must be Reggie," she says, and offers her hand like Reggie is some business acquaintance.

He looks tentative at first, but then he puts his hand out and shakes.

"Violet's told me a lot about you," my mother says.

Ding! And there it is. That's how long it takes for her to say something embarrassing—and not even true. I haven't told her a lot about him. As a matter of fact, I've told her as little as possible about him.

"Not really," I butt in, trying not to get mad at her in front of Reggie.

"It's okay," Reggie says.

"Of course it's okay, Violet. She says such nice things about your family." My mother seems more self-assured than she usually is when she has to deal with new people.

"Okay, Mom," I say. I want her to leave before she says anything else.

"You two have a good time. I have to get back to work."

The minute she leaves, I try to defend myself to Reggie. "I didn't really say all that much."

"It's okay," he says again.

"It's not."

I could explain more, but I leave it at that.

Even though Reggie's visit to my house doesn't start well, we end up having a pretty good time. We spend most of the afternoon at the kitchen table side by side coming up with plans for the treehouse. He is pretty impressed with my drawing abilities, and I am pretty impressed by the way he throws around building terms like *cleat* and *2 x 4* and *joist*.

● ● ● ● ● ● ● ● ● ● ● ●

"Reggie wasn't anything like what I thought he would be," my mother says at dinner. "Are you going to have him over again?"

"I guess."

"He seems sweet. Maybe I *should* meet his mother. Does he take after her?"

"Not really," I say, thinking about cool, confident Mrs. Walker.

"He must a little. After all, she's his mother."

"You don't have to meet her," I say, pushing away my plate of half-eaten food.

"I thought you wanted me to."

I shrug.

She's right, I did want her to meet Mrs. Walker in the beginning, but now it's worked out well, having two separate spaces—my everyday world and the Walkers' world next door. I don't want anything to change.

# Eleven

THE next morning Mom reminds me that my dad is picking me up at three. "Make sure you do your homework while you're there," she says. "Don't wait until you come home."

"I won't, Mom," I say. "I'll get it all done."

When I go next door, Reggie's sitting in the backyard by himself looking through my sketches of the treehouse. Yesterday we decided that we can start putting together the support beams from some pieces of leftover wood in the garage.

But since no one else is outside with us, Reggie first wants to show me where in the woods he plans to put the treehouse. We wind our way through the trees. The spot he's chosen is easy to get to, but far enough away from the house that when we're high up, no one will be able to see us.

"Remember, I've never used a hammer," I say, looking up at the tree trunk and wondering how the two of us will actually manage to construct this treehouse.

"Don't worry about the hammer," Reggie says. "I know what I'm doing."

We're working our way out of the woods when we hear Chloe shout, "I'm going outside now, Mom!"

"The real problem is going to be how to keep this a secret from my family and keep Chloe out of our hair," Reggie says as we emerge into the backyard.

Chloe is sitting by herself, kneeling in the grass holding a chalkboard. Two dolls sit on small plastic chairs in front of her.

"No, Tiffany, that is incorrect," she says, wagging her finger at one of the dolls. "Anastasia? No, no, that's not right either. Why haven't any of you been listening to me?

"Hi, guys," she says to us. "Wanna play? You can be students in my class."

"We're doing something else," says Reggie, walking away from her.

"Rose and Daisy are running an errand with Dad, so you have to play with me, Reggie. Or just Violet can play with me."

"No way," he says.

"I have an idea. Maybe you can help us," I say as Chloe gets up from the grass, ready to do battle with her brother. "We have this project," I explain.

Reggie raises an eyebrow.

"We're going to build a treehouse."

"Uh," Reggie says. "What she means is—"

I interrupt him. "We're going to put it in the big oak in front of the house."

"The one you ran into?" she asks.

"Yeah. Maybe you could come up with some design ideas."

"Really?" Chloe says.

"Sure," agrees Reggie, catching my drift. "Go draw something for us."

"Tiffany and Anastasia, are you listening? We have to go inside to do something very important. If the two of you don't cause any problems, you can watch me," she says to the dolls. Then she picks them up and sticks them under her arms like footballs and marches toward the back door.

"If you tell her we're going to build a treehouse in the front, she'll never think about looking for it in the back," I say. "And we don't have to hide what we're doing in the garage. And then at some point, we just tell her it didn't work out and distract her with something else."

"You're more devious than I thought," Reggie says. "In fact, that will work for anyone in my family who asks. Dad won't care about the lumber—he's let me use it for other projects."

He looks pretty pleased with me, and I feel pretty pleased with myself. It's not often that I come up with a smart idea that I'm actually able to put into words at the right time.

Reggie pulls open the garage door. The Walkers use one side for parking and one side as a work area. There are tools hanging on a pegboard, different-sized pieces of wood stacked and leaning against the wall, and a scratched-up worktable. The design we are thinking about for our structure is simple, based on a website we found called Backyard

Forts DIY. We'll use wide planks for the floor of the fort and some shorter pieces for the support.

"Let's get started," Reggie says.

"What if Chloe hears us and wonders why we're starting without her plan?"

"We'll just tell her we're making the floor, which is the truth."

I hold two of the boards together while Reggie hammers. He's careful to make sure my fingers are out of the way before he bangs on the nails. We work slowly and steadily, and I can already picture our final product. We'll decorate it with old rugs and a makeshift table and maybe a glass bowl that I can salvage from our kitchen. We can put flowers in it and have a box of our favorite books. I can even leave some pencils and drawing pads up there.

I'm lost in my thoughts when I hear a voice in the driveway call, "Hello?"

"Is that your mother?" asks Reggie.

He goes out to see, and I follow him.

"Reggie," my mother says like she's surprised to see him, even though she's standing in his driveway. "I thought I would stop by and finally meet your mother. Is she here?"

"I think so," he says.

We both know his mother is inside. Reggie hesitates for a moment and then heads toward the back door.

"I'll get her for you," he says.

My mother looks happy with herself, but I'm mad.

"I told you that you didn't have to come," I say.

Before she can answer, Reggie appears from around the back with Mrs. Walker following him. Chloe's right behind her mother with a cookie in her hand.

"So nice to finally meet you," says Mrs. Walker, thrusting her hand toward my mother. "I'm Sabrina Walker." Mrs. Walker is wearing a plaid button-down shirt and jeans. If you saw her from a distance, she could pass for a high school student.

My mother doesn't step toward her but leans in so she can shake hands. "Eva Crane."

"And I guess you met Reggie just now," says Mrs. Walker. She removes her hand from my mother's grip and immediately places it on Reggie's shoulder.

Reggie pulls away. He doesn't volunteer the fact that he was at our house yesterday, and neither does my mother.

"And this is Chloe," says Mrs. Walker. Chloe shoves the rest of the cookie in her mouth and stares. I wonder if she is critiquing my mother's outfit, her sweatshirt and matching sweatpants that used to be black but are now a washed-out gray: Too baggy, no fun, could use some color!

"I've heard so much about your whole family from Violet," says my mother. Then she just stands there, shifting her weight from side to side. She doesn't seem to know what else to say.

"How nice," says Mrs. Walker.

"Yes," says my mother. She's starting to look like she

regrets whatever extraordinary impulse landed her here: stuck face-to-face with the perfectly composed Mrs. Walker. "Anyway, I was just on my way home from the store and thought I would stop by."

"Would you like to come in?" Mrs. Walker says, gesturing at the house, although even I can tell from her tone that she doesn't really want my mother to come in.

"No thanks. I can't." My mother is starting to get that antsy energy she has when she's nervous.

"Are you sure?" asks Mrs. Walker.

"I'm on my way home from the store."

"So you said," says Mrs. Walker.

The more uncomfortable my mother looks, the more in control Mrs. Walker seems.

"I need to get the groceries out of the car and put away. But some other time," says my mother as she heads for the path between our houses.

"She's weird," whispers Chloe.

"Don't be rude," says Mrs. Walker.

While we watch my mother take the bags out of our car, Mrs. Walker says, "I'm so glad to finally meet your mother. Too bad she couldn't come in."

"I bet she could have come in," says Chloe.

"Chloe, please," says Mrs. Walker. The two of them head inside.

"She's really nice. Your mother," says Reggie when we're back in the garage.

"I guess. And weird, just like Chloe said."

"I like her."

When I get home, my mother is in the kitchen pouring hot water from a kettle into a mug. She's changed out of her sweatshirt into a clean white T-shirt and has pulled her hair away from her face with the red headband I wore in last year's class picture. With her hair pulled back, I notice the similarities in our faces: our eyes are big and gold-flecked and a little too close together, and our lips are thin, with a downward tilt to them.

"I can see why you want to be at the Walkers' so much. It seems like there's a lot going on," she says.

"I don't want be over there that much," I protest, although I think about how I have been there almost every day since they moved in. And how Reggie and I have just started a new project there that may take some time to finish. And how, after we finish the treehouse, we're probably going to want to use it together all the time.

"It's fine," my mother says. She removes the tea bag from her mug and takes a careful sip. "I'm glad you have a new friend. You should get ready for your dad. He'll be here any minute."

 # Twelve

"IS my hair really that thin?" my father asks on Sunday morning.

We're sitting in chairs on the patio outside his apartment. He's reading the paper and drinking his coffee, and I'm sketching him. Mrs. Moses announced we could pick whatever we want to do for our first art project, and I've decided to do a series of portraits.

"I'm still working on it, Dad," I say. I get out the dark brown pencil and add a little more color to his hair so that he doesn't feel bad.

"So, how was the first week of school? How are your teachers?"

"They're fine. My homeroom teacher's really nice," I say.

"That's good," he says, putting the paper down. "How about we go for a walk in the park before I take you home?"

"Sure."

When Dad drops me off, Mom has already started making macaroni and cheese, which is my absolute favorite dinner. It's her way of apologizing. She must have felt bad for the way her visit to the Walkers' house went.

After dinner we sit together on her bed and watch some TV show that we both can't help laughing at, even though we know it's stupid. We both like to watch something mindless on Sundays to distract ourselves from the fact we'll have to get up early in the morning.

■■■■■■■■■■■

When my alarm goes off, I get dressed and get my books together. Then I grab a piece of toast on the way out so that I won't be late meeting Reggie, especially since Mrs. Walker has decided that the two of us should go to the bus stop on our own this week.

Reggie and I had agreed to meet at the top of the Walkers' driveway at 7:40, but when I get there, he's nowhere to be seen. I wait for a few minutes, finishing my toast and kicking the dirt at the edge of the Walkers' property.

Mr. Walker removed some low bushes and planted trees in the spot so that they will give the house more privacy when they get bigger. The dirt beneath the trees is still dark and fresh, and even though the wind barely blows, the fragile young trees sway a little. It's still early in the day, but it's already warm and the air feels thick and suffocating. My shirt sticks to the skin underneath my backpack, and little beads of sweat start to gather on my forehead.

Still no Reggie. I start to worry about missing the bus. I hate being late. As a matter of fact, I hate being late so much that most times I can't stop myself from being early. I even keep a book and my pencils and a sketchbook in my bag so that I can pretend that I arrived early to my destination in order to accomplish something.

I'm sure Mrs. Walker would drive us to school if we missed the bus, but I don't really want her to. I head toward the house to hurry Reggie up myself. The back door's already open a crack, so I pull it just a little more and poke my head into the mudroom.

"Her mother was a little strange," I hear Mrs. Walker say to Reggie.

I can't see them, but they must be in the kitchen. I picture the two of them sitting at their gleaming table, a vase of wild-flowers displayed in the center.

"Just like Amanda Simon said when I had coffee with her last week," Mrs. Walker continues. "It's fine for Violet to come here, but just don't go there." I hear her push her chair in and turn the water on to do the dishes. She's probably put on those big yellow gloves she keeps under the kitchen sink so that her hands can stay soft.

"Too late," Reggie says.

He's speaking loudly, and I can tell from his tone that he's mad.

"What do you mean?" Mrs. Walker says.

"I've already been there," I hear him say. "Last Friday after school."

"You lied to me?" she asks. "I thought you went to Owen's."

"I didn't lie. I just never said where I was going."

"It's the same thing and you know it. You need to ask me before you go to someone's house, Reggie."

"It wasn't *someone*. It was Violet," he says.

"I think my judgment is a little better than yours in this case. And I'm still not sure why you won't consider playing with Owen. It might even be more fun than playing with Violet. More like what other boys do."

"So?" Reggie says.

"So," she says. "You know what, Reggie? I don't feel like arguing with you now. Just stay at our house, that's all. We'll find some other friends who might be more appropriate for you. I want you to be a real part of things here. Anyway, now's not the time to talk. You're going to be late."

I feel myself flush. The heat is coming from within—like something deep inside me caught on fire and there's no way to put it out. My heart pounds and my legs are shaky. I back up, wishing I could run away. Instead, I stand motionless in front of the Walkers' door, my face warm and clammy. I'm still there, trying to make myself breathe again when Reggie emerges.

"You're here," Reggie says, putting his backpack on and tightening the straps.

"I'm here," I say.

Am I here? I don't feel anywhere right now. I feel suspended in time—still hearing Mrs. Walker's icy tone ring in my head.

"Sorry I'm late," he says.

My stomach is in knots as I think about the conversation. Mrs. Simon told Mrs. Walker that my mother is strange. Mrs. Walker thinks my mother is not an appropriate host for Reggie. Mrs. Walker thinks *I'm* not appropriate for Reggie. How could I have been so stupid? Why did I think the Walkers liked me so much? Why did I think I was fitting in so well? If only my mother hadn't stopped by.

Reggie is more talkative than usual on the way to the bus stop. He doesn't seem like someone who's had a big fight with his mother. He goes on and on about his idea for this month's art project. He's building a birdhouse that he's going to paint and decorate. During the bus ride, I listen to him talk, but no matter how hard I concentrate I only hear half of what he's saying.

I'm relieved when the bus finally pulls into the school driveway.

He gets off first but stands on the sidewalk waiting for me. "See you after school?" he says.

I don't want to go to the Walkers' house today. I don't want to go to the Walkers' any day.

Another bus drops off a load of kids and the sidewalk is starting to get crowded. The two of us aren't moving, so people maneuver around us, trying to get to the front door.

I stare at my feet.

"Hey," says Reggie. "Are you tired or something?"

"I don't know. Maybe." I pick up my feet and force myself toward the door.

"After school?" he asks again. "You'll come over? Work on the treehouse?" He looks concerned, like Goldie does when she's sitting by the door watching everyone go outside without her.

I remember how Reggie said "It was Violet" to his mother, like I was something special. Like I was a real part of his world.

"I guess," I say, following him into school.

I can't tell Reggie that things have changed and that I no longer want to spend time with the Walkers. Or actually that things have changed and now I don't want to *be* a Walker. Or, what's more important, that I know the truth: no matter how hard I try, I never could really be one of them.

∎∎∎∎∎∎∎∎∎∎∎∎

"I've got a great idea!" says Katie when I walk into homeroom. She grabs me by the shoulders and spins me around so that we're facing each other.

"Geez, hold on," I say. "Let me put my stuff down."

Rachel is standing next to Katie, who is now jumping up and down like she does when she gets excited. She's always gotten excited a lot, and very quickly. When we were younger and I went to her house, her mother was constantly reminding Katie to think before she acts. I remember some of the things we did together, and I guess Katie's mother was right. Like once in the wintertime, Katie had a great idea: we would make the floor of the Pattersons' backyard shed into an ice-skating rink by dumping water onto it and letting it freeze. Or another time when we decided to decorate her family's car with stickers that we had collected. Sometimes her plans could get you into trouble.

"What is it?" I ask as we head toward our seats.

"The intramural soccer tournament!"

"You can take Rachel's place on our team!" Katie says triumphantly. "Rachel was going to play, but she found out yesterday after school that she got a big part in her dance production, so now she can't."

"My mother says I can't risk getting a soccer injury now," says Rachel. "Not after I got the lead in *Swan Lake*." Rachel throws her arms out in front of her with a dance-y flourish, her elbows gently bent and her long fingers touching.

Katie doesn't bother responding to Rachel because she can't wait to give me the details. "It's only two days. Today is the scrimmage, and tomorrow is the real thing. They're busing us over to the extra fields next to Meadow Pond because our fields are already being used."

"I'm not sure," I say.

"I have two pairs of shin guards with me, and they have buses that will bring us back to Franklin after school. All your mother has to do is pick you up here at six," says Katie. "It's all settled. You are officially a member of the Franklin Jelly Beans."

"The what?" I ask.

"Missy is our captain, and it was her idea for the team name. We're all going to wear jelly-bean-colored shirts," says Katie. She jumps up and down again. "I'm so happy you're going to do it! It's going to be so much fun. Now we have to get Ms. Santorini to let you call home so you can get your mother to give you permission."

"I don't think I can today. I already have plans to go over to Reggie's house," I say, even though the thought of those plans makes me feel clammy and warm all over again.

"Just tell him you're doing this instead. He'll understand."

"I don't know."

"He won't care," says Katie, even though she doesn't know Reggie at all. "Go to his house some other day. You can tell him at lunch.

"Ms. Santorini, Violet has to make a phone call!" Katie shouts at the top of her lungs.

"Violet, is that true? Does it need to be done now?"

"It's about after-school soccer," explains Katie.

"Katie, I believe Violet is capable of speaking for herself. Isn't that true, Violet?" asks Ms. Santorini.

I nod and say, "Yes, I do have to call my mother."

"Make it quick," Ms. Santorini says as she begins to take attendance.

I feel a little silly asking to use the office phone, but that's the school rule. Even though you have a perfectly adequate phone in your pocket, you can't use it on school grounds during school hours.

The office secretary taps her fingers on her desk while I make the call.

"Mom?" I say as I stand at the counter.

"Violet? What's wrong?" She sounds worried. "Are you okay?"

"I'm fine."

"Then why are you calling from school?"

I understand why she's confused. I don't think I've ever called her from school myself, and I only went to the school nurse one time in elementary school, when my third-grade teacher could tell from feeling my forehead that I had a high fever.

"Is it all right if I go to intramural soccer at Meadow Pond after school today? They have buses that bring us back to Franklin, so you'd just have to pick me up from school at six. They emailed you a form."

"I don't remember seeing it."

"You need to fill it out now for me to be able to do it," I say. "Just look."

"Is Reggie doing it, too?"

"No, but Katie is. She asked me to be on her team."

The school secretary sighs loudly.

"Why didn't you tell me you wanted to do it before this?" My mother has gone from surprised to annoyed.

"Katie asked me just now," I say.

"She should have asked you earlier."

"Well, she didn't."

I don't want to think about the fact that Missy, Katie, and Rachel were all planning to do this tournament, and no one had said anything to me. Maybe they didn't think I was a good enough soccer player to be on the team, but Rachel isn't exactly a soccer star, either. Although I guess Rachel has qualities that I don't have. Like I bet if Rachel had rammed into a tree on the Walkers' makeshift soccer field, she would have gotten up gracefully and stood straight and tall.

"All right, fine," says my mother. "I'll sign you up."

# Thirteen

AT lunch, I scan the cafeteria for Reggie to tell him that I can't go to his house this afternoon, but he's nowhere to be found. After lunch, as I stand in the hallway with the rest of my class, I finally spot him, waiting in line.

"I looked everywhere. Where were you?" I ask.

"Ms. Moses let me eat lunch in the art room today so that I could start my birdhouse project. I spent the time figuring out the design, and she's letting me use some supplies in the art room," he says. He looks happy and relaxed, although that fact hasn't changed his position in his class line—he's in the back in his usual spot. Everyone else is paired up, but he stands by himself, swinging his lunchbox gently back and forth.

"Mr. Walker, there is no talking in the hallway right now," says Mrs. Schein, who has identified him with the eyes in the back of her head that everyone says she has. "I know this rule is not observed by most teachers. But I believe that a few moments of quiet meditation after we eat is a helpful habit for all of us to maintain."

He shrugs at me and stares down at the floor.

"Reggie," I whisper. I need to quickly tell him that I'm not going to his house this afternoon because of the tournament. I'm glad to have a real excuse, a believable excuse, for not going to the Walkers' house.

"Excuse me, young lady," says Mrs. Schein. She has somehow walked to the back of the line without us seeing her. "Whose class are you in?"

"Ms. Santorini's."

"Then I believe your class has left you behind," says Mrs. Schein. She gestures ahead to the last couple of kids filing into our classroom. "Perhaps you should join them."

"But—"

"No *buts*. Please return to your class."

I walk away just in time to see the last person in my line go in, so I jog a little to catch up.

"No running, young lady," calls Mrs. Schein from behind me.

I can't stop thinking about how I didn't tell Reggie that I won't be on the bus and that I won't be going to his house this afternoon. I wish I had been able to talk to him, because then I could try to put the whole thing out of my head.

Instead, all kinds of questions and doubts swirl around inside me. Maybe I shouldn't have agreed to play with the Jelly Beans, especially since they only asked me to the join the team at the last minute. Maybe I should have made myself go to Reggie's house despite what his mother had said. Maybe it would have been better to go and to pretend that everything is okay, that everything is the same.

In between each afternoon class, I search for Reggie. Even with the threat of punishment from the eagle-eyed Mrs. Schein, I'm determined to talk to him, but I don't see him. While I'm usually happy when the last bell rings, today it just reminds me of what I haven't done. I stand there and watch for Reggie out the window during dismissal—kids who are going home head straight for the buses, and after-school kids stay in the classroom so that they don't slow things down in the hallway. I finally spot his backpack at the end of a long, zigzagging line of kids. He's really not that far away from me, but there's no way I can go outside to tell him. Somehow, in my uncertainty about everything, I don't even think about texting him.

"Lucky it's just practice, so it doesn't matter that you're not wearing soccer shoes," says Katie, who has come over to stand by the window with me. "Tomorrow, though, you should wear them."

I'm wearing my regular sneakers, and I don't have soccer shoes. I should tell Katie this, but I don't. I don't think soccer shoes will make any difference in how well I play. The buses pull out. There's a blob of color that might be Reggie sitting on our bus. He must be sitting alone. He must be wondering about what happened to me. Maybe he'll think I went home sick.

"If you are playing in the intramural soccer tournament, please proceed to the front of the building. Your bus will meet you there in a few minutes," Ms. Santorini announces.

I turn away from the window and follow Katie out. When Katie and I arrive at the double doors, Missy is already outside waiting with three other girls from her class. Owen, Jake, and three other boys I don't know are standing next to them. The teams have to be co-ed, and Missy must have recruited them for the Jelly Beans.

"Guys, listen!" shouts Missy. "I have our shirts." Then she turns to me. "I don't know if Rachel's shirt is going to fit you, Violet. It might be too small."

"It'll be fine," says Katie.

I wonder if Katie had to ask Missy for permission before she asked me to take Rachel's place. I wonder if Missy tried to find someone else but couldn't and that's why Katie asked me this morning instead of texting last night.

"Does everyone know their position?" asks Owen. "I'm going to play center, and Missy and Jake are forwards. Katie, you said you want to be goalkeeper, right?"

"Yeah, well, I don't really love to run," says Katie, grinning.

Jake laughs, but Owen frowns at her.

"You're going to be serious, right?" he says.

"Sure," says Katie. She gives Owen a flirty smile, and he looks a little more forgiving.

"Rachel was playing defense. That's what you'll have to play," Missy says to me.

"You'll be right near me," Katie says, putting an arm around me. It makes me feel better, a little less awkward standing here.

"Listen up," says Mr. Fletcher, the gym teacher, as the bus pulls in. "When we get to Meadow Pond, let's get everything in place quickly so that you guys have the afternoon to practice. Today is just a scrimmage, and then we will have our game day tomorrow. Tournament winners will be treated to a pizza lunch at the end of the week, courtesy of J and J's Pizza."

"Let's do it, Jelly Beans!" shouts Missy.

Owen punches his fist into the air, and the rest of our team cheers.

By the time the bus arrives at Meadow Pond, the sun that was so bright and hot this morning is nowhere to be seen. Instead, a big black cloud hangs over the field.

"According to the forecast, the rain is supposed to hold off," says Mr. Fletcher. "But it's another reason to get out there and make the best use of our time. The elementary school is using the Meadow Pond field, so Sharks and Tornadoes will be playing on the field behind it, and Hornets and Jelly Beans on the one farthest from the school. Let's get out there!"

As we run past the Meadow Pond field, I see Rose and Daisy stretching next to each other on the side of field.

"Hey, Violet!" shouts Rose, waving at me. Her hair is pulled into a ponytail, with a blue terrycloth headband holding the blond tendrils off her face. She's sitting with her legs spread out into a wide V.

"What are you doing here?" asks Daisy when I stop next to them.

"Intramural soccer tournament."

"Why didn't you tell us you were going to be here?" says Rose.

I shrug as Katie yanks at me. "Violet, c'mon," she says. "We better get going or Missy is going to be one sour jelly bean."

When we get to our field, everyone is putting on their shin guards. Katie hands me the extra pair from her backpack. Missy has already distributed our shirts to everyone else, so next to the red-shirted Hatchets are nine kids in assorted fruit-colored shirts. Did Missy not understand that team shirts are usually all the same color? Missy's shirt is a Day-Glo pink that looks great against her tanned arms, while the rest of the team is wearing shades of yellow, green, and blue.

"These are yours," says Missy, handing me a cream-colored shirt and Katie a pretty lime-green one.

"What kind of jelly bean is this?" I say, holding up my shirt.

"Coconut," Missy says. "Rachel asked for it specially." When I put it on, it blends so closely with my skin tone, I'm almost transparent.

"Everybody ready?" shouts Owen from the middle of the field. He's wearing a cobalt-blue T-shirt that accentuates his dark hair.

Katie puts on her goaltender gloves and waves for me to accompany her down to the end of the field. Missy won the coin toss, and Owen already has the ball. I'm relieved when he moves aggressively down the field, away from me. The Hornets and Jelly Beans are well matched. Mostly the centers and midfielders kick the ball back and forth, trapping the ball in the center. As we play, the clouds over us darken, and the wind starts to pick up.

The plays ricochet back and forth on the field, but no one has scored. The ball has been kicked at me twice, and each time I've been able to punt it down the field, away from our goal. They weren't exactly precise kicks, but they did the job. A couple of raindrops land on my arm.

"Oh, man, here comes the rain," says Katie.

I look back at her and nod.

I'm half turned around when I realize that the ball has been catapulted down the field and is not too far from me. A boy who's about twice my size charges at me. I use the same footwork I've been practicing when I play with the Walkers to steal the ball, but this time my feet are slow and clumsy.

"Violet!" I hear Katie shout behind me.

I try to tap the ball out from under the boy's foot, but at the same time he changes his feet up and forcefully passes the ball to the other side of the field. That Hornet player takes aim and as Katie throws her body to the other side of the goal, he plants it in the back of the net.

Katie picks up the ball. She looks heartbroken.

"One–nothing!" shouts a Hornet.

"Oh, c'mon," I hear Owen shout from midfield.

"Sorry," I say. I wait for Katie to say something, too.

"Don't blame Katie," Missy says. "*Violet* should have had it."

"Whatever. Let's go, Jelly Beans!" shouts Jake. "Jump, jump, jump like a bean," he sings.

"Yeah, it's all right," says Katie, mimicking Jake's enthusiasm. "We can still do it." Then she gives the ball a forceful kick to the middle.

"Teams off the field!" shouts Mr. Fletcher.

"What???" shouts Owen.

"We have ten more minutes," says Missy.

"Nope, I'm calling it now so that we can get in before the rain starts. Everyone will need to wait in the gym for our bus to arrive. And listen up—there will be some elementary school kids waiting in there as well, so mind your manners," says Mr. Fletcher.

We follow Mr. Fletcher off the field.

Katie and I walk behind Missy and Owen, who are strategizing for tomorrow's game.

"Hey, Katie, come on. We need our goalie in on this," says Owen.

"Okay." Katie speeds to catch up with them. Then she turns back to me and calls, "Violet, come on."

"That's okay," I say. "You go ahead."

As I watch her, I hear Missy say to Owen, "It's too bad Violet had to take Rachel's place."

"Yeah, it stinks," says Owen.

I try to keep my eyes on the ground, but I can't help noticing Missy loop her arm through Katie's as they all put their heads together to work on a plan.

●●●●●●●●●●●
●●●●●●●●●●●

Rose and Daisy are standing in the middle of the gym.

Daisy spots me standing near the door and motions me over to them.

"It's so cool that you're here!" says Daisy.

"Did you win?" asks Rose.

"Nah," I say.

"Oh, man," says Daisy, scrunching up her face. "What was the score?"

"Zero to one. But it was just a scrimmage and we quit early because of the rain."

"Still," says Rose.

"That's okay," says Daisy. "You'll do better tomorrow."

"If I go tomorrow."

"You've got to go," says Rose. "Your team is counting on you. Don't be a quitter. When Reggie quit baseball, he messed everything up."

"What do you mean?" I ask.

"He played on a traveling team for two years. But there was this one game when he made some mistake and walked off the field. Then he just gave up and never went back. My mother says she should have never let him quit."

"Rose!" says Daisy. She gives her sister an annoyed look.

Suddenly, I remember that I never did reach Reggie. I

could've texted him after school or on the bus to the soccer field, but I forgot.

I take my phone out of my hoodie pocket and see that there's a text from Reggie. There's no real message, just a single question mark. I text him back and explain that I couldn't come over because I was at the soccer game.

I wait for him to respond, but he never does.

 Fourteen

BY the time the bus to Franklin arrives, the rain is really coming down. I'm last in line, so when I reach the bus door, my shirt is soaking wet. Katie, Missy, and Owen have found seats in the back of the bus so I sit by myself and am happy to see that my mother's car is waiting in the parking lot when the bus arrives at Franklin.

I run over to the car and slide into the passenger's seat.

"How was the game?" my mother asks as we drive away.

"Fine."

"Just fine? After all that?"

"After all what?"

"Nothing." She doesn't say anything else to me the whole ride home.

●●●●●●●●●●●●
●●●●●●●●●●●●

The first thing I do after I walk into the house is take off my shoes, shin guards, and red sweatshirt. The color from my sweatshirt has run, and the coconut-colored T-shirt is stained with uneven pink lines. I know that Missy will not like this new design. I picture myself explaining tomorrow on the field that it's a strawberry-coconut jelly bean.

That's it, says tomorrow's Missy. *You're off the team.*

Don't listen to her, says tomorrow's Katie.

It's fine, says tomorrow's me. *I didn't want to play anyway.*

Today's me wonders how it would be to be someone who didn't need to rehearse what they'll say in conversations with their so-called friends.

I go to my room to change, wishing there was some way to peel the whole afternoon from my skin.

I crumple up my T-shirt, shove it under my comforter, and put on a pajama top. Even though it's only dinnertime, I feel like I could go to sleep right now.

I'm sitting on my bed when my mother knocks softly at my door.

"You know, Reggie came here looking for you today," she says.

"He did?"

"He thought you were sick. He even brought you some of his mother's cookies."

"Why would I want those if I'm sick?"

"Really?" she asks, and then she pauses like she wants me to take back what I said, but I don't.

"You don't have to worry about the cookies," she finally says. "We ate them."

"What do you mean *we*?"

"When I told Reggie you were at the soccer game, he stayed for a bit."

"Didn't you have to work?"

"He didn't stay very long, and he needed the company. Next time you make plans, you should really tell him if you aren't going to be there."

"I know that."

"It's not very nice."

"I *know*. I tried to tell him at school, and then I forgot to text him until after the game."

"You could go over there and apologize."

I point at the clock.

"It's almost their dinnertime."

I picture the Walkers at the table. I picture going into their kitchen and confronting Mrs. Walker—Mrs. Walker, who thinks I'm not good enough, who thinks my mother is not good enough—and I know there's no way I can do it.

"Maybe they're eating late tonight," suggests my mother.

"You don't understand," I say. "Mrs. Walker has a schedule."

"Things come up. I'm sure they don't eat at the same time every night."

Suddenly I am furious. At Mrs. Walker for talking to Reggie about my mom, and at my mom for introducing herself. "Why are you telling me things when you don't really know? You don't know anything about the Walkers."

My mother looks at me and shakes her head.

"I might not know about them, but I do know something about you, Violet. And I know that you've gone overboard about these people."

"I have not!" I shout. "Why do you think you know me?"

"I think being your mother counts for something," she says, turning around in the doorway. She seems strangely calm, and it only makes me angrier.

"Maybe it shouldn't," I say.

"Oh, Violet," she says quietly. "That's not very nice."

"Maybe I'm not nice!" I shout.

"We should talk about this when you're calmer. Maybe you're hungry. I'm going to make dinner for us."

After I sit through a quiet dinner with my mother, I write Reggie another lame text telling him how I'm sorry and explaining again that the Jelly Beans needed me for their team. I hope he'll just text back with an *I get it* and then we can just pretend that everything's fine. I check my phone every ten minutes until I go to bed, but he never answers. I turn the lights off to go to sleep, but my thoughts keep me awake.

I feel terrible for not remembering to text Reggie and hurting his feelings; I feel terrible for all of the things I said to my mother. I just feel terrible, and I know I can't sleep until I make at least one of them right. I get out of bed and creep into my mother's room to apologize to her, and even though she's usually up late, tonight the light's already off and she's got the covers pulled up over her chin. I stand by the side of the bed and gently jiggle her arm to wake her up.

"Are you sleeping?" I ask.

She grunts.

"Are you not talking to me?" I say, pulling at her again. "Please, Mom. I can't take both you and Reggie not talking to me. I didn't mean what I said."

"I know that," she says, sitting up. "It's fine."

"It's not fine," I say, clutching her arm.

"Okay, but *we're* fine," she says, hugging me. "Just go to sleep, Violet. In the morning, you can talk to Reggie, too, and you'll clear this whole thing up."

■■■■■■■■■■■

I want so badly to clear things up with Reggie that the first thing I do when I wake up is check my phone again, but there's still nothing from him. As I get dressed, I think of my two options for the day. After school I can play soccer with people I don't really like or I can go to the Walkers' house—that is, if Reggie is still talking to me *and* if I can stand to hang out at a house where I'm not really welcome.

Somehow being with people I don't want to be with seems better than being someplace where people don't want me to be. But even if I can't force myself to go to the Walkers' house, I know I need to talk to Reggie. I leave the house early so that he doesn't head to the corner without me. When I reach the

Walkers' driveway, TJ is still standing there with his headphones on listening to music.

TJ glances at his phone and then takes his headphones off.

"You know Reggie's not going to be out here for fifteen minutes, right?"

"I guess," I say. "But aren't you late for your bus?"

"Jack Simon's picking me up," he says. "Reggie said he was feeling sick last night, so he might not even be going to school. You should knock on our door and make sure he's going."

"That's okay. I'll just wait here."

TJ punches some numbers into his phone.

"Mom? Violet's waiting for Reggie.... Okay. I'll let her know." He hangs up and tells me, "Lucky I was here. He's staying home today. You still have a lot of time. You should probably go home."

"You're right."

After I leave, I turn around to watch him. TJ has put his headphones back on and is listening to music, his head bobbing up and down to the beat. If you saw TJ now, you would never know that just a few minutes ago I was standing right there next to him. One minute I'm there, the next minute I'm gone and he's back in his own world. If I never showed up again, I wonder if any of the Walkers other than Reggie would even notice.

I don't want to go in and face my mother, so I stay on the porch steps with the spiders. On the day Reggie came over, he had noticed the webs—the ones that I had left untouched on the porch after my momentary impulse to destroy them had evaporated. Reggie went on and on about how fantastic spiders are and how even though spider silk looks delicate, it's actually incredibly strong. He said that it's so strong that people use it when they make things like airbags and helmets, and he added how unbelievable it is that such a small creature can produce something that has the power to protect us.

●●●●●●●●●●●●

At lunch, all Katie and Missy want to talk about is today's tournament and how the pizza lunch at the end of the week will be so fun if we win. I can tell that Rachel is annoyed because she keeps trying to change the subject back to her dance performance. Katie tries to include me in the conversation, but I can't gather up the energy to do more than nod at them.

After school, we sit with our own teams on the bus to Meadow Pond. Mr. Fletcher stands at the front next to the bus driver as he reads the rules of the game. Sometimes when the bus hits a bump, he has to grab the top of the seats so he doesn't go flying.

"Same matches as yesterday. Game one, Sharks versus Tornadoes on Field Two and Hornets versus Jelly Beans on Field Three. After that, winners play each other and whoever wins that game gets the pizza prize. Any questions?"

"How much pizza do we get when we win?" asks Owen.

"No way you're winning," says Maria, the Hornets' captain.

"Don't worry. We'll save a few scraps for you," says Owen.

"Let's not get ahead of ourselves, people," says Mr. Fletcher. "Team captains, see me when we get off the bus."

Our team stands together by the bus, and everyone puts on their shin guards while Missy meets with Mr. Fletcher.

Jake puts his arms out straight, palms against the bus, and stretches his quadriceps. Katie looks at him and starts to jog in place.

"Don't you want to warm up, Violet?" she asks. "Oh, shoot, you forgot your soccer shoes."

I look down at my feet as if I were making a discovery.

"That's okay. You'll be fine without them," she says.

"Jelly Beans, front and center," Missy shouts. "Everybody put your shirts on and let's get to this. Same positions as yesterday!"

I take my still-damp T-shirt out of my backpack and unravel it. The red streaks of yesterday have been absorbed into the cotton, turning it an unattractive grayish pink. It looks like what has happened when my mother is preoccupied and washes all the clothes together instead of separating the darks and the lights.

"Nice shirt," says Owen.

"That was supposed to be coconut," says Missy.

"Now it's strawberry-coconut," I say, but it comes out lame.

Katie giggles, and she doesn't seem to notice that Missy isn't laughing.

I try to remember what else I was going to say to today's Missy, but my mind goes blank. As I put the shirt on over my tank top, I try not to breathe in its musty scent.

No one scores in the first half of the game. During the second half, our offense pummels the Hornets. Owen, Missy, and Jake take turns scoring and after ten minutes we're up 4–0. The ball never even gets to my end of the field.

After the game, we line up with the Hornets.

"Good game, good game, nice game," say my teammates as we proceed down the row of Hornets. I mutter it along with everyone else, but my heart isn't in it. Since I barely touched the ball the whole game, I feel a little phony participating in this ritual.

"Jelly Beans and Tornadoes, you're up," shouts Mr. Fletcher. "The team that wins will be our champion!"

Missy and the rest of the team throw their arms around each other as they march down the field chanting, "Jellies! Jellies!" They are way more excited about this than I am.

In the first fifteen minutes of the game, Owen scores two goals, so we're ahead 2–0 at the beginning of the second half. When we switch sides, I look over to the sidelines. While we were playing, a bunch of mothers, including Mrs. Simon and Mrs. Patterson, arrived and set up folding chairs on the edge of the field.

"How did your mother know we were going to make it to the final round?" I ask Katie.

"She didn't. She just wanted to come to support everyone. Does your mother have to work today?" she asks.

"Yeah, she's got a big deadline," I say.

"Too bad," says Katie.

"It's fine. I'll tell her about it later."

Fifteen

WHEN Mr. Fletcher blows the whistle for the end of the game, our team goes wild. Katie runs from the goal and hugs me. I should be happy because we won. I even helped by getting the ball to Owen so that he could make one of our goals.

"Woo-hoo!" screams Missy from the center of the field. She motions to Katie, who lets go of me and runs straight at Missy with her hands up. They high-five, and then they run together to the side of the field. Mrs. Patterson grabs both Katie and Missy and envelops them in a big hug. Owen walks right by his mother to join them. The rest of the Jelly Beans and the Tornadoes move toward the side of the field, merging into one big mass of kids and parents.

Instead of joining my teammates, I start walking off the field toward the bus. No one stops me. A few kids who got antsy watching the last game are milling around near the buses talking, so I stand awkwardly next to them. When the bus driver decides to open the door, I get on.

I could sit anywhere, but I pick my usual seat a few rows from the front. It seems like the best place to be as inconspicuous as possible. Not that I need to worry about that, because everyone else is still outside, wallowing in defeat or reveling in victory. And not that many people will be on the bus anyway, because so many parents showed up and will drive their kids home. I'm glad that I don't have to talk to anyone. Not one piece of me feels happy that my team won, probably because I don't feel like I'm part of them.

I get my pencils and sketchbook out of my backpack to keep myself occupied for the ride back to Franklin.

Usually, the good thing about drawing is that even when you're not in the mood to be creative, you can draw what's right in front of you, but today I'm not even in the mood for that. By the time we reach the Franklin parking lot, all I've done is doodle a long chain of boxes that cover the page.

●●●●●●●●●●●

My mother picks me up from the school.

I tell her we won, and she's happy. But it's clear that I don't really want to talk about it, and she doesn't push me. She lets me turn music on instead.

When we pull into our driveway and I get out of the car, Rose and Daisy are already home and in their yard.

They must have seen us pull in, because Rose shouts, "Violet! Come over!"

I pretend that I don't hear her.

"I think maybe you should go over and say hello," says my mother.

I don't feel like getting into another argument with her, so I force myself to head next door to the Walkers'.

When I approach them, Rose says, "After-school ended before your tournament was over. Did you win?"

I nod, and she raises her hand to give me a high five. Reluctantly, I meet her hand in the air.

"We should celebrate," says Rose. "Maybe you could come to dinner?"

"I have too much homework," I say. "Besides, isn't Reggie sick?" There is no way I am going into their house.

"Not really. Our mother just let him stay home. She wouldn't ever let us do that, but he's different," Rose says, making a face. "I think she's worried that if he goes to school in one of his moods, it will make him some kind of outcast. Like he was at our old school."

"Rose!" says Daisy.

"What?" Rose says. "Violet doesn't care. Anyway, it's true."

"He's fine now," says Daisy. "It helps that he met you—that he has a real friend now."

●●●●●●●●●●●●●

When I leave the next morning, Reggie's already standing on top of his driveway waiting for me. He's fanning himself with one of his notebooks because it's another scorcher. It shouldn't feel like summer anymore, but it does.

"I saw your text about the soccer tournament," Reggie says. "You know, you could have just told me you'd rather do that than come over."

"The Jelly Beans didn't ask me until after you and I had made plans. I tried to tell you, but then Mrs. Schein made me go to my classroom before I could, and then I forgot to text you after school."

"It's okay, Violet. I get it."

Reggie's tone is so understanding. It makes me wish even more that I could be honest with him and tell him that I overheard what his mother said about me. But how can I tell him that I don't want to go to his house ever again because now I know the truth?

We don't talk for the rest of the walk or even while we're standing at the corner. When the bus comes, I get on first. I sit down in our regular seat, and Reggie sits down next to me just like he always does.

It's so hot that every window on the bus is open, and the only thing saving us all from suffocating to death is the small breeze we get when the bus is in motion. I pull my sketchbook out of my bag even though I don't feel like drawing, and Reggie takes out his bird book. When I look over his shoulder, he's studying a picture of a yellow-bellied flycatcher, a small bird whose body and head look like they are almost the same size. If it had been a sketch instead of a photograph, I would have thought the person drawing it had gotten the proportions all wrong. I don't try to talk to him about it—or anything else—on the ride to school or even when we're heading together down the Building B hallway.

Before we break off to go to our own homerooms, Reggie does stop, though. Our eyes meet, and for a moment I think he's going to say something, but he just waves goodbye instead.

●●●●●●●●●●●●
●●●●●●●●●●●●

"Guess what?" Katie says, and then she grabs me and enfolds me in a hug as she jumps up and down, making me jump along with her. "Ms. Santorini says that because the air conditioner is broken in the cafeteria, we get to eat lunch outside today."

"Isn't that awesome?" says Rachel.

"That's great," I agree.

"Let's get the spot under that tree near Building C," says Katie.

Even though it's only been a week, the monotony of school has already settled in, so the morning classes drag by. Everyone is thrilled that the air conditioner isn't working—and that we get this unexpected break in our routine. When it's time for our class to head out to lunch, the playground and fields are swarming with overexcited kids.

"Let me have your attention!" shouts the cafeteria monitor. With her authoritative voice, she seems like a military commander barking orders at her troops. "Your boundaries today will be the baseball fields. Anyone who is found going beyond those fields will end up with automatic detention.

Remember that lunch outside is a privilege. At the end of the period, all garbage must be picked up and placed in the proper receptacles. Is that understood?"

Some kids fall into place and reply "Yes, ma'am" with their loudest and best soldier impressions. Most just ignore her and wander away, concentrating on the bigger mission: searching for the best lunch spot.

"Missy, we're here! We're going to the Building C tree!" shouts Katie, signaling frantically across the playground to the other classes. When Missy joins us, she tucks her arm into Katie's. Rachel tucks her elbow under Katie's other side, and I trail behind them.

"C'mon, Violet," says Katie, turning her head to make sure I'm there.

When we reach the tree, Rachel puts her back to the trunk and starts to slide down. Her posture's so perfect, she could probably balance a stack of books on her head as she descends. But as she almost reaches the ground, she stops and squeals. We all look and see a long line of ants right next to Rachel, marching from the tree into a large cone-shaped anthill.

"Ewww," says Rachel. "Gross. I'm not sitting anywhere near that."

"Me either," says Missy, kicking up the dirt and showering the ants with a cloud of dust.

"Don't!" I shout. "Leave them alone."

"They're just ants," says Katie.

I stand next to the tree. I've never been a particular fan of ants, but right now I can't stand the thought of them being pelted with dirt. There they are, just leading their normal ant lives, when all of a sudden their world is being turned upside down by someone else, by something they can't control.

"Maybe you should sit with them," says Missy.

"Maybe I will," I say.

"Ewww," says Rachel again.

"What's wrong with you these days, Violet?" Katie asks.

"What's wrong with *you* guys?" I reply.

"I'm out of here," says Missy, grabbing her things.

"Me too," says Rachel. "C'mon, Katie."

"We don't need to kill them, but I don't exactly want to sit in them, either," says Katie. She follows Missy and Rachel.

I sit down in the grass and let myself lean against the tree. The dust settles, and the ants position themselves back into a single line, marching one behind the other. Their collective path is straightforward now, as if the world makes sense to them again. I draw my legs up, put my head down on my knees, wrap my arms around my shins, and watch them. In the distance, I can hear the sounds of everyone else screaming and playing and having fun. I could go and try to be a part of it, but it feels far away, and I can't get myself to move. Maybe I'll stay next to the anthill, under this tree, forever.

"Hey," says a voice.

When I pick my head up, there's Reggie, standing right in front of me.

"I was looking for you," he says. "You okay?"

"Sure, I'm fine."

"I saw your friends walking that way," he says, gesturing toward the school. "Where are they going?"

I point. "They don't want to sit near a bunch of ants."

"Oh," he says.

"Or me," I say, my voice breaking a little. Reggie's looking at me with such care that it's hard to pretend to be fine.

"They wanted you to be on their soccer team," he says, sitting down next to me.

"I'm not sure about that. Anyway, I'm pretty sure I'm not cut out to be on *anyone's* team."

"How about mine? I mean, it's not the best, but still. Guaranteed snacks and dog-time," he says, trying to make me smile.

"I don't think so." I would like to be on his team, but I can't. Not with Mrs. Walker's tone of disapproval reverberating in my head.

"Why not?" Reggie asks. He's given up trying to joke and is now staring at me with a solemn expression on his face.

"I just can't," I say.

"Why not?" he asks again. "I don't get it."

"Because."

"Because *what*, Violet?"

"Because I overheard her," I blurt out. "Your mother." The words come out of my mouth short and cold and sharp.

Reggie plucks a piece of grass like he's going to make

one of his special grass whistles, but instead of bringing the blade to his mouth, he plays with it—passing it carefully from one hand to the other.

"She doesn't want you to be friends with me," I add.

"That's not it," he says, tearing the grass in his hand. "Don't you get it?"

I look at him and wait.

"*I'm* the problem. It's me. She wants me to be like TJ and Rose and everyone else in my family. She tells everyone that it's okay that I'm not like them, but that's not what she really thinks."

He looks so sad. I feel even worse for making Reggie feel bad.

"I shouldn't have said anything. You don't have to tell me," I say. I can't look him in the eyes, so I pluck a piece of grass, too, just to have something to concentrate on while he talks.

"No, I want to," says Reggie. "I want to tell you."

I nod and he continues.

"She keeps wanting me to make a new start here. Back in our old neighborhood, she couldn't stand it that I wasn't popular like TJ. When she went to my baseball games, she was so embarrassed that I wasn't really friends with anybody. I hated when she came to those games. Once I screwed up and dropped a ball that was an easy catch, and when I looked over at her, she had her hands over her eyes like she couldn't bear to see me. I got so mad that I walked off the field."

"That stinks," I say.

"After that, everyone on the team started calling me Walk-away Walker, so I quit. Those guys were such jerks. But all she wanted me to do was be friends with them. And now that's all she cares about again."

"That's not fair," I say.

"You're lucky your mother's not like that," Reggie says, turning his attention to the ant that has started crawling up his arm. He drops the blade of grass and carefully removes the ant from his arm, transferring it to the very tip of his index finger. Then he stands up and deposits the helpless thing right on top of the anthill. Reggie's ant starts moving again and quickly grabs the opportunity to join the stream of other ants, scurrying away from the two of us—the two of us who were only trying to protect it—and escapes, burrowing into the path that leads deep into the ground.

Sixteen

"**HI,** guys!" shouts Chloe when Reggie and I start down the Walkers' driveway.

"Why are you home?" asks Reggie.

"Mom picked me up early for a doctor's appointment. See, they give out stickers and lollipops when you get a shot at this doctor," she says, pointing to a pink pony sticker that she's wearing on her dress. She's sitting on the steps of the front porch with a stack of papers and crayons spread out next to her. "And look, while I was in the waiting room, I worked on my design for the treehouse."

Reggie and I sit down on the steps next to her, and she scrunches in close to me. Her body is warm, and her hair smells faintly of candy. Chloe looks so happy to see us that I stop thinking about how I told myself there was no way I was ever going to spend time at the Walkers' house again. After what Reggie told me at lunch today, I couldn't say no when he asked me on the bus if I'd keep working with him on the treehouse.

Chloe hands me a piece of construction paper. In purple crayon she has drawn a mini-mansion. The only treehouse-like thing about it is that there's a tree trunk that runs through the middle of it.

"That's a piano," she says pointing at a black block on the second floor. "Can you help me draw it better?"

"No problem," I say, accepting the crayon she hands me.

Reggie looks over my shoulder as I rework the outline of the piano.

"That may be a little complicated to build," he says.

"Don't worry. If we work together, we can," Chloe says. "I have to change out of my school clothes so I can help, and then I'll get some cookies and stuff for us." Chloe jumps up and heads toward the back door.

While we wait for Chloe and the cookies, we talk about our art projects for school. Reggie is telling me about how he wants to use pieces of metal he found in the garage for the roof on his birdhouse, and I explain that I have portraits of my mother and father already drawn for my art project, but that I want to do more.

My mother's car pulls into our driveway, and if I squint, I can see her heading up the walk to our house. She has a large grocery bag in her arms, but she puts it down on the porch. I think she's stopping to get her key out when she turns around to face the Walkers' house. I wonder if she's looking for me.

"There's your mom," says Reggie.

"Yeah," I say.

"Hi, Mrs. Crane!" shouts Reggie. He waves his arms furiously at my mother. "Maybe we should go over there and show her Chloe's design."

"Why?" I ask.

"She'd think it's funny, too," he says.

"Nah," I say.

"C'mon, let's go." He grabs Chloe's design out of my hands and heads off to my house through Goldie's path. "Mrs. Crane! Wait! We thought you might want to see something funny."

"Okay, well, I was just going in," says my mother. "Do you want to come inside?"

Reggie turns back and looks at his house. No one is outside yet.

"We can just show you here," he says.

Reggie sits down on the top step of the porch, and my mother sits down next to him. They're about the same size, and their heads are almost touching as they examine Chloe's picture. I'm still standing, but neither one of them seems to notice or care.

"It's my sister Chloe's idea for a treehouse she wants us to build," he says, handing the paper to my mother so that she can see the details.

"Wow, is that a piano?" she says with a laugh. "She sure dreams big."

Just then, I see Mrs. Walker at the top of our driveway and hear her shouting Reggie's name.

Reggie doesn't move.

"I think your mother must need you for something," says my mother. "Maybe you should go."

He nods, but he doesn't move toward his mother. Mrs. Walker starts slowly down our driveway. She is wearing white pants, a blue button-down shirt, and her favorite clogs.

"What did I tell you, Reggie?" Mrs. Walker says. She's only halfway down the driveway, so she has to raise her voice to be heard.

I thought I would boil over the next time that I actually saw Mrs. Walker, but I don't—I feel numb. I watch as she very deliberately walks toward us, step by step; it seems like she's walking slowly in order to make Reggie squirm.

My mother doesn't wait for Mrs. Walker to reach us. Instead, she approaches Mrs. Walker with Chloe's drawing still in her hands. Reggie follows behind my mother, but I stay back on the porch.

"I'm so sorry to bother you," Mrs. Walker says.

"No bother," says my mother. "Reggie just came over to show me something."

Mrs. Walker smiles at my mother and then turns to Reggie. "That's very nice, Reggie, but Chloe said she was taking cookies outside for you and Violet and then she couldn't find you. Remember I asked you to tell me when you are going somewhere."

Especially when you are going to the weirdo neighbors, I think.

"I was right here," explains Reggie.

"I see that," says Mrs. Walker. Her voice gets even more strained. "But remember that we talked about this."

If we weren't here watching, she would be meaner, I think. *She'd say what she really thinks.*

"Violet, how are you?" says Mrs. Walker, looking past Reggie and my mother, as if she's just noticed me.

Before I can answer, my mother says, "You'll have to excuse me. Groceries." She points to the bag on the porch. But as she turns around, she smiles at Reggie and hands Chloe's design back to him. "Thanks so much for sharing this."

"So is it okay if Violet comes over like she and I planned?" Reggie asks his mother.

"Mrs. Crane might want Violet to stay at her own house," she says. "Though, of course, we'd love to have her."

"You can go, Violet. Just don't overstay your welcome," my mother admonishes me.

"She couldn't do that," Mrs. Walker adds sweetly. "We really do enjoy having her. Chloe's waiting, so why don't you two come with me now?"

Reggie and his mother don't say a word to each other on the way back to their house. Chloe's standing on the front lawn. She's changed into a green-striped shirt and purple shorts, and she's brought out a plateful of cookies, a large container of milk, and some paper cups.

"Make sure things go back into the kitchen later," Mrs. Walker says sharply. "That will be your responsibility, Reggie."

"Look, guys, I brought out the rest of my art supplies, too," says Chloe.

"We'll talk later, Reggie," Mrs. Walker says as she heads into the house.

Reggie and I sit down under the tree with Chloe. I pour the milk, and Reggie distributes the cookies onto three napkins. In between bites, I add a chandelier to the family room in Chloe's picture, and Reggie suggests digging a swimming pool in the flat grass next to the treehouse. We work for a long time without talking much.

When Chloe gets bored and goes inside, Reggie and I move into the garage. Reggie clears the workbench so that we can put together the support beams. Mrs. Walker doesn't come out again. Instead, when it's dinnertime, she sends TJ to get Reggie. I'm happy to have made it through the rest of the afternoon without seeing her.

●●●●●●●●●●●●

"I thought we'd have spaghetti tonight," my mother says when I walk into the house. "And breadsticks. Just like at the diner, right?"

"Great," I say. Even though it's pretty basic, I can't get enough of my mother's spaghetti. She always buys this special sauce that's got lots of basil in it, and I love basil.

"Did you start building that crazy treehouse that Reggie showed me?" my mother asks as she stirs the sauce.

"No, we didn't. I mean, that's not something we're *really* going to do. It's just…"

I don't want to give away anything about our real project. Now, more than ever, I like the idea of our treehouse being a secret. It will be a place where both Reggie and I can be out of his family's way.

"Just what?" my mother asks, watching me.

"Nothing."

Even though Reggie obviously likes my mother, I don't think he would want her to know about our plans. And I definitely don't want to take the chance of upsetting him again by opening my big mouth.

My mother looks disappointed.

"It doesn't matter," I say. "It's just too complicated to explain."

"That's okay. I get it," she says. She turns back to the stove and concentrates on stirring the sauce.

# Seventeen

IN morning homeroom the next day, Katie asks me if I want to take the bus with Missy to her house after school. Missy and Katie are going to make Franklin Soccer Tournament Commemorative T-shirts, and they want me to design them.

"Maybe you could draw a jar of jelly beans in a soccer goal or with a big first-place ribbon on it," Katie suggests.

"I can't come over today," I say. "I've got other plans."

"With Reggie?" she asks.

●●●●●●●●●●●●

By the time the afternoon bus ride is over, Reggie and I have the next steps we need for the treehouse all figured out. The floorboards and the support beams are already complete, so today we can start assembling everything out back. I text my mom to tell her that I'm at the Walkers'.

"We just have to walk Goldie first," Reggie says as we approach the house.

"I'll wait out here," I say as Reggie heads in the back door.

After a few minutes, Reggie comes out with Goldie. "TJ isn't around and Rose and Daisy are at after-school. Mom's going to the bus stop soon to meet Chloe. I told her not to expect us back from Goldie's walk for awhile, so we could start building. We can move the wood when she goes to get Chloe."

We wait by the side of the house until Mrs. Walker leaves. Reggie hands me Goldie's leash and begins to drag the floorboards and supports into the woods. He makes a couple more trips, and then we head back to the site together, where he ties Goldie to a nearby tree.

"Sit, Goldie. Good girl," Reggie says.

Goldie looks at him adoringly and plops herself down. She rests her head on her paws.

"We'll put a ladder up the side later," Reggie says. "For now, just climb up like I do."

He grabs on to a thick branch with both hands and shimmies up with his feet. Then he pulls himself onto the branch, swings his feet over it, and sits.

"Now hand me those pieces and come up the same way I did. I'll keep going up to that next branch."

"Okay," I say. I reach out to give him the short planks we nailed together earlier, and he rests them in the crook between the trunk and the branch.

"Be careful," he says.

I follow while Reggie reaches up with one hand and clings

to the trunk with his other hand. The tree trunk is gnarled and has lots of bumps and ridges, which help with climbing. He cautiously sits down on the higher branch and steadies himself by holding on to the edge of a small hole in the tree trunk.

"Here's a handhold. Right here," he says, pointing.

"Okay, I'll try." I'm getting a little nervous, wondering if I'm strong enough to do what he just did.

He starts to pull himself up again by grabbing another branch and sticking his hand farther into the cavity to get a better grip, and I see a bee fly out. Then there's another and another. I watch as five or six bees emerge from the hole and swarm around Reggie's head and arms. He takes his hand off the branch to bat the bees away.

"Owww!" he yells.

As he swats at another bee, Reggie lets go of the branch—and seems to fall in slow motion. His arms flap, like the wings of an injured bird, but the rest of his body floats by, strangely flat and motionless. Then I hear him land right beneath me with a horrible thud.

"Reggie!" I shout. "Are you okay?"

When he doesn't answer, my heart begins to thump wildly and my entire body shakes. As I shimmy my way down, I peer through the space between my legs and see his body splayed out on the ground. Goldie is desperately trying to reach him, too, but the rope around her neck pulls taut.

When I finally get myself down to the ground, he isn't moving.

"Are you all right?" I ask again.

Goldie stops barking the minute I reach Reggie, and my voice echoes in the quiet of the woods. Goldie must think we're playing some kind of game, because now she's wagging her tail at us, probably hoping that we'll untie her so that she can be a part of it.

"I—I guess," he sputters.

Very carefully, he pulls himself up and sits in the triangle of dirt between the roots of the tree. He leans back, letting the rutted surface of the trunk support him, and I breathe out, relieved. According to Chloe, who loves to tell a good Reggie disaster story, Reggie's fallen from trees before. In the past, no matter how hard he fell, he's never even broken anything. One time when he was climbing a tree in the yard in front of their old house, he reached for a branch, missed, and did a perfect somersault in midair, landing right on his feet.

"I need to rest for a minute," he says.

We sit side by side while Reggie tries to get his breath back. He closes his eyes, and I notice a red welt appear on his cheek and then another on his forehead. Then there are a couple that emerge just below his knee and some more on his forearms.

"Reggie, look," I say, pointing at his arm.

He opens his eyes and examines himself, holding his arms out in front of him, watching red patches appear. It seems so strange—these red bumps traveling along his skin and puffing up.

"Do they hurt?" I ask.

"No, they're just kind of itchy," he says, rubbing at one on his leg.

Then he rubs at his eyes, and his whole face flushes red. At that moment, he goes from his normal self to something else. It's like whatever's happening inside him takes over, and Reggie can't do anything to stop it.

"I don't feel so well," he says, and then he closes his eyes again.

His body crumples, and he lays flat on the ground with his head touching the bottom of the trunk.

"What's wrong?" I ask. He doesn't answer me, so I shout, "Reggie!"

I'm right in his face, leaning over him, but he's not moving and he's not saying anything. I shake him gently, but he still won't answer. I rest my hand lightly on his face as though my touch could somehow make the color disappear, but of course it doesn't. For a moment, I'm so scared that I can't think. Then something shifts in my brain, and I know what's happening.

"I'm going to get your mom. I'll be right back," I say, and then I start running. I charge through the woods, going as fast as I can, dodging the tree roots and branches along the path. At the back door, I hesitate for just a second. Then, I push the door open.

"Hello!" I shout into the mudroom.

"Violet? Is that you?"

I step inside and look into the kitchen where Mrs. Walker is standing at the sink looking toward me and Chloe is sitting at the table with a large glass of milk in front of her.

"What's going on?" asks Mrs. Walker. "Is everything alright?"

"It's Reggie," I say.

"Reggie?"

"He needs help."

"I thought you were out walking the dog. Where is he?" she asks.

"Back in the woods. We were working on our fort—"

"In the woods? Without me?" Chloe interrupts.

I ignore her and continue, "He was climbing a tree, and—and..."

"Did he fall?" asks Mrs. Walker.

I nod.

"Let me get bandages," says Mrs. Walker. She opens the cabinet and finds her medical bag.

I grab her by the forearm. "I don't think that's what he needs. He was stung by a bunch of bees. He's having a reaction."

"What? How do you know?" she asks.

"My mother's allergic to bees too, and she's explained to me what it looks like so I could help her if I had to. She has an EpiPen, just in case."

Mrs. Walker quickly turns around and heads toward the door. From the mudroom she shouts back to Chloe, "You stay right here! I'm going with Violet."

"But, Mom!"

"Do what I say, Chloe!"

I run past Mrs. Walker and she follows me. When we're outside, I hear her call 911.

"It's my son," she says. We head past the big rock and into the woods. "He's had an allergic reaction. Yes, that's the address. No, it's never happened before. No, no, I don't have one.

"Violet, call your mother!" yells Mrs. Walker after she gets off the phone. "Tell her to bring her EpiPen."

Mrs. Walker and I reach the place where Reggie is lying on the ground, and I pull out my phone. Goldie is barking wildly, but she stops when she sees Mrs. Walker.

"Oh, no," says Mrs. Walker, stooping down next to Reggie. His eyes are still closed, and he's wheezing.

I call my mother. As soon as she answers, I say, "We need your help."

"What? Where are you?" asks my mother.

"In the woods behind the Walkers'. Come now! Bring your EpiPen!"

"Why?"

"It's Reggie! Just come!"

The line goes dead.

Mrs. Walker turns to me. "Is your mother...?"

"She's coming," I say.

Mrs. Walker gets up and heads to a spot where she can see my mother through the trees, and I crouch by Reggie's side.

He's making funny noises. It sounds like he's trying to say my name, but I'm not sure. Hearing him so weak and raspy only scares me more. I grab his swollen hand. I need a sign, a sign that under his swollen face, the usual Reggie is still there. I squeeze his hand and I want him to squeeze me back just a little, but he doesn't; his fingers are limp inside mine.

Goldie is suddenly on all fours, barking. I hear twigs cracking and footsteps pounding on the dirt.

"We're back here!" Mrs. Walker shouts, waving her arms.

Now there's my mother in a white sweatshirt, coming through like a light from the green shadows of the woods. She got here so quickly; she must have cut through on Goldie's path. Her hair is flying in all directions and a few leaves cling to the side of her hair. In her right hand, she has a tube that she hands to Mrs. Walker.

"Thank goodness," Mrs. Walker says.

I stand up and get out of the way as Mrs. Walker grabs the tube and kneels down next to Reggie. She takes the EpiPen out of its tube, removes the safety cap, jabs the point into Reggie's thigh and holds it there, counting out three seconds.

As she's doing that, my mother moves to Reggie's other side. "I'll try to get the stingers out. That could help," she says, taking Reggie's hand and scraping her fingernail along the skin.

After giving the injection, Mrs. Walker puts the cap back on and drops the EpiPen on the ground. Then, she just sits there. It's almost as if she can't move. "Look at me, I'm a nurse, but I don't know what else to–to do . . ." she stammers. "I can't even think straight."

"Why don't you put your sweater under his feet? To help with the blood flow," says my mother.

"Right," says Mrs. Walker. "Right."

She takes her sweater off and gently places it under Reggie's sneakers. As soon as she does, Reggie starts to shake a little—first his hands, then his legs—and I get scared again.

"It's the medicine. That can happen," my mother explains. She's done with Reggie's hand and has come to stand by my side. "It's just the medicine working."

"I'm scared," I say.

My mother puts her arm around me, and I lean into her.

After a few long minutes, Reggie's shaking starts to ease up. Mrs. Walker strokes his hair with one hand and holds his hand with the other. Every few minutes, she tilts her head to the side and gets down close to him, so that she can listen to him breathe.

"Can you hear me, Reggie?" asks Mrs. Walker. "I think he can," she adds, smiling a little. "He squeezed my hand."

"Please, please be okay," I say.

The three of us watch as Reggie's wheezing starts to diminish, and his whole body seems to relax. I untie Goldie so that she can sit next to him, too. I feel sure that her warm body pressed against his will make him better. The red spots are still puffy, but the swelling has begun to go down. He looks like Reggie again.

"He's going to be okay," says my mother.

"He is," says Mrs. Walker, turning to my mother, "thanks to you."

My mind starts racing, envisioning all of the terrible endings to the story of this day.

"What if you hadn't been at home when I called?" I blurt out.

"Not much chance of that," my mother says, and then laughs.

"C'mon, Mom." I don't want her to make fun of herself, not now. "If you hadn't come so quickly, I don't know..."

But I do know—I just can't say it. *It all could have turned out so differently.*

"Can you hear me?" Mrs. Walker asks Reggie again.

This time, Reggie nods and opens his eyes.

"What happened?" he whispers. Then he notices me standing behind his mother. "Violet, what happened?"

"Don't you remember? Climbing the tree for our fort back here?"

Both my mother and Mrs. Walker look at me and wait to hear more.

"This was our getaway plan. It was going to be a secret spot for our treehouse—a place for us to run away to," I explain.

"Oh, I see," says my mother.

I wonder if Mrs. Walker understands, too, but she doesn't say anything.

Reggie's eyes open wide, as if it's all coming back to him.

"Now our plan won't work," he says quietly.

"No," I say.

"But it doesn't have to," declares my mother, hunching down next to Mrs. Walker to talk to Reggie. My mother's shirt is streaked with dirt now, and her hair's a mess, but her face glows with a faint pink color. "Reggie, you're such a brave kid—you've already got the hardest part down, being yourself," she says. "You don't worry about what anyone else thinks, so you don't need to run away. Really, there's a lesson there for all of us," she adds. "Even me."

My mother pats Reggie's leg and returns to my side. She doesn't say anything else, but she puts her arm around my shoulder and pulls me toward her. I can hear the siren of the ambulance getting closer.

Then Goldie starts to bark again when the ambulance pulls into the driveway.

"I'll tell them where you are," says my mother.

"Thank you," says Mrs. Walker. She turns to me and asks, "Violet, could you run inside and stay with Chloe? And take Goldie with you?"

I really don't want to leave Reggie, but I nod, grab Goldie's leash, and follow my mother out of the woods.

She approaches the EMTs who are standing in the driveway and quickly explains what's happened and leads them back toward Reggie.

I peel away from the group to take Goldie inside.

When I open the door, Chloe is sitting on the floor in the mudroom. Her face is streaked with tears.

"It's okay, Chloe," I say. "Reggie's going to be fine."

"But there's an ambulance," she says. "I heard it."

"There is. But he's all right."

"Are you lying?"

"No, it's the truth. My mother had medicine that helped him."

Goldie and I sit next to Chloe. None of us moves until we hear Mrs. Walker's voice in the driveway. When she hears her mother, Chloe runs outside and I go after her. Reggie has an IV attached to him, and he's on a stretcher that's being loaded into the ambulance. Mrs. Walker and my mother are talking to an EMT.

Chloe throws herself at her mother.

"Everything's okay, Chloe," Mrs. Walker says, hugging her.

"So why is Reggie on a stretcher? Why does he have to go to the hospital?"

"Just to make sure the medicine worked completely," Mrs. Walker says. "But he's going to be fine."

"We're going now," says the EMT to Mrs. Walker. "Would you like to ride in the back with him, ma'am?"

"Yes, of course," she says.

"I want to go, too," says Chloe.

"No, you stay with Violet and her mother until TJ gets home," Mrs. Walker says, and then she turns to my mother. "If that's all right with you?"

"Sure," says my mother.

"I'll call TJ from the ambulance and explain," says Mrs. Walker. "My husband can pick him and the girls up and then meet me at the hospital."

"It's no problem. Chloe can stay at our house for as long as you need," my mother says.

Mrs. Walker grabs my mother and holds her tightly. She keeps on holding until it looks like she's never going to let go. Finally, she pulls herself away. "How can I begin to thank you?" she asks.

"It's really okay," my mother says. "Anyway, no need to thank me, because Violet already considers you family."

"She's not really our family," says Chloe.

"Chloe!" says Mrs. Walker, exasperated.

"Chloe's right," I say. "But we are friends. That's enough."

Eighteen

THE ambulance leaves with Mrs. Walker and Reggie, and my mother and I make our way toward our house with Chloe trailing behind us.

"So, what would you like to do?" my mother asks Chloe.

"Maybe we can play school," I say.

"I don't want to play that," Chloe says. "I'm scared for Reggie."

"It was scary, but he's going to be all right," says my mother.

When we get to our house, Chloe opens the door in front of us and rushes in. She doesn't stop at the living room but heads straight down the hallway.

"I found your room!" says Chloe, and then she goes in to look around.

From the top of my dresser, she picks up a diorama I made in third grade. It was supposed to be a model of my room.

I had painted the inside blue, even though my walls were and still are white, and had used bits of yellow eyelet to make curtains as a substitute for the blinds on my real windows. The only accurate detail is the stack of books I had made to rest on the little nightstand. I had painstakingly written the names *Ramona the Pest* and *Alice in Wonderland* on the flimsy cardboard spines. On top of that stack was a pad labeled "Violet's sketchbook."

"I want to make one of these," says Chloe.

"Okay, it's not hard," I say. "It just takes some patience."

"Great, you two have a project!" says my mother, who has come to check up on us. "I have to get back to work."

"I'm going to make one as a present for Reggie," says Chloe.

"I bet he'd love that," I say.

"It can be a model of my room. I can make little drawings of the posters on my wall."

"Maybe you should make a model of Reggie's room. You know, if it's a present."

"I guess," she says. "Even though his room isn't as nice as mine."

We find an old shoebox, and Chloe and I work together on designing Reggie's present. As Chloe makes paper replicas of Reggie's bed and nightstand with a miniature *Birds of the Northeast* guidebook sitting on top, I picture Reggie's blotchy face after he was stung by the bees. Chloe is busy trying to re-create Reggie's room, but all I can think about is how his family would have felt if something had happened to him. If all that was left of him were his possessions.

There's a loud knock at the front door.

"I bet it's TJ," says Chloe.

"Bring your present with you," I say, heading to the door.

"But I'm still working on it. I don't want to go," says Chloe, trailing behind me with the diorama in her hands.

"Hey, Violet, thank you," says TJ. He has a serious look on his face that makes him seem older than usual.

"No problem. She was fine," I say, giving Chloe a little push toward him.

"Not for Chloe. My mother told me what happened. Reggie might be dead if it wasn't for you."

"Not really."

"*She* didn't do it," says Chloe. "Violet's *mother* saved Reggie."

TJ shoots Chloe a look.

"She's right. It was my mother," I say.

"Okay, thanks to both of you, then."

TJ grabs Chloe by the shoulder and says, "C'mon, Dad dropped me and Rose and Daisy off and has left for the hospital. We need to get home now."

"But Violet and I were working on Reggie's present. See?"

"Let's go, Chloe," says TJ as he leads her back next door.

After dinner, I sit on the living room couch with my pad and pencils on my lap. I pretend to draw, but all I really do is stare out the window. The Walkers' house is unnaturally bright this evening. I imagine Mr. and Mrs. Walker are both at the hospital and that the four Walker kids at home must have turned the lights on in every room, exposing what's going on inside the house to anyone who might be walking by.

"Violet," my mother calls from her room.

I leave the window to find my mother.

"Mrs. Walker called me from the hospital," she says. "Reggie's going to be just fine. They're discharging him later tonight, so when you come home from school tomorrow, he'll be ready to see you."

"But I want to skip school and stay with him," I say.

"He'll probably be exhausted in the morning."

"So?"

I know that I won't be able to concentrate—that there will be no point in going to school—until I see Reggie at home, next door, where he belongs.

"He might not be up for much talking or anything."

"He doesn't have to talk," I say. "I just want to be with him."

"I don't know," says my mother, but I can tell that she's giving in. "I guess I can call Mrs. Walker and check."

"Please call her."

"Maybe it would be better for him to just be with his family," she says. "And don't you have that big soccer celebration lunch tomorrow?"

"I want to be with Reggie. I know you understand. Please, Mom."

"All right, I'll call."

In the morning, I don't wait. I don't care that it's early or that TJ and everyone else may still be eating breakfast. I don't care that Reggie's probably not even awake yet. I don't care what Mrs. Walker will think of my getting there so early. All I know is that I need to see for myself that Reggie's really okay.

As I jog through Goldie's path, yesterday's events flash in front of me. Reggie's falling body, my hand on his, my mother coming through the woods with the EpiPen. The flashing ambulance lights, the serious but kind voices of the blue-coated EMTs. Mrs. Walker's contorted face after she stabbed Reggie with the EpiPen, looking like she wanted to pick him up and to cover him with her own body at the same time.

I reach the Walkers' backyard. Even though it's early morning, there aren't any crows on the rock. Usually there are scraps of food on the rock from breakfast leftovers, but Mrs. Walker hasn't fed the birds today. I knock on the door, and Mrs. Walker opens it so quickly, it's almost as if she had been peering out the window waiting on the other side just for me.

That's not normal, but this is not a normal day. Mrs. Walker doesn't even look like herself; she's pale and drawn, like what happened yesterday has wrung all of the color out of her. And Mr. Walker is sitting at the table, his fingers laced around a coffee cup. He's never there in the mornings during the week. When I walk in, all of his attention turns to me.

"Violet, you know that we can't thank you enough. You and your mother."

Some other day I might be embarrassed. I might turn red and feel the need to say exactly the right thing in response to Mr. Walker's praises. But not today. Today is not normal for me, either. I don't smile out of embarrassment when Mr. Walker thanks me, and I don't feel the urge to add anything to the conversation. I don't care about being polite, because I'm on a mission.

"Can I see him?" I say instead.

"He's in his room," says Mr. Walker.

"I don't know if he's awake," Mrs. Walker says, keeping pace with me as I run out through the kitchen door. When I get to Reggie's door, she stands in front of it, like a guard. "Violet, hold on."

I can't believe that Mrs. Walker is stopping me now. I can't believe that she won't let me see Reggie with my own eyes.

"Hold on," she says again. "You can't go in there until..."

I'm concentrating so hard on what I need to do that I bite my lip. If she doesn't hurry up, I think I'm going to have to make a break for it and run behind her.

"Until I say something," she finishes.

I wait there while she stares at me. She looks me up and down, like she's seeing me for the first time.

"I just have to tell you that I was so, so frightened when I saw Reggie on the ground there yesterday," Mrs. Walker explains, her hands clasped in front of her. "I was so frightened that I might lose him."

Of course, I know this. And I don't know why she's

stopping me to tell me, but I decide that I should try to be nice if it will get me to Reggie more quickly.

"Yeah," I say. "I was scared, too."

"There's more. I owe you an apology, Violet. Reggie told me that you overheard our conversation a few days ago about you and your mother."

"It doesn't matter."

"It *does* matter. To you and to Reggie," she says. "He was so upset with me, but I insisted I was right to say what I had said, that I was just trying to protect him. I was listening to him, but I just didn't understand. I couldn't really hear what he was saying."

"Just like Reggie with the yellow warbler," I say.

"What?" she asks, looking confused.

"Never mind."

"Anyway—when I saw him under that tree—" Mrs. Walker breaks off and crosses her hands over her arms as if she's trying to hold herself together. She stays frozen in that position: her head dropped, her chin against her chest. She seems so sad that I reach out to her. When I touch her shoulder, she grabs on to me. She pulls me in closer, and I put my arms around her. Through her sweater, I can feel the back of her rib cage—her ribs feel bony, sharp, breakable.

"You're a good friend, Violet," she says, pulling away. "You're the kind of friend Reggie needs." And then, without adding anything else, she steps out of the way.

Reggie's in bed with his eyes closed. His head is propped

up on two pillows, and his body is tucked tightly into a crisp white cotton quilt. Chloe sits on a folding chair that's been placed next to the bed. In her hands she has the diorama of Reggie's room, the one we made yesterday, and her art supplies are stacked at her side.

"Just keep your eyes closed, and I'll tell you a story before I have to go to school," she says to Reggie. "Okay?"

Reggie doesn't respond.

"What story are you going to tell him?" I ask Chloe from behind.

"Violet!"

I know she's being very careful, because she shrieks quietly.

"What are you doing here?"

"I'm just checking in," I say.

"On me?" she asks.

"On Reggie."

"He's really tired," Chloe says, making a face because she can't hide her disappointment. "He's even too tired to look at the present that I made him. Mom says not to bother him."

"I guess she's right."

"That's why I'm telling him a story. That's no bother," explains Chloe. She hands me one of her pencils and some paper. "While I tell my story, you can draw him. For one of those portraits for that project that Reggie was telling me about."

"Good idea," I say, looking past her to Reggie, who hasn't moved at all.

With shaky hands, I start to sketch Reggie, trying to

capture the expression on his face. He's breathing quietly and evenly, his upper and lower lips not quite closed together. And even though his eyes are shut and he's not taking part in the conversation, he seems alert, observant, like he is when he's awake. Reggie may choose to stand on the sidelines, but my mother's right: he's brave, because no matter where Reggie stands, he only pays attention to what matters.

I'm as silent as he is, listening to Chloe's *very* detailed story about a beautiful, magical fairy princess named Chlorinda Walking who saves her family and the entire kingdom from death and destruction, but my hands are steadier now because I feel sure that I can be brave, too.

Nineteen

KATIE, Missy, Rachel, and I head out to the yard after lunch. When I pull the heavy door open, I shiver a little. It's finally starting to feel like fall.

Reggie, Mrs. Schein, and Ms. Moses are already outside, standing in a semicircle a few yards away. They've positioned themselves around a large tree whose leaves have just started to turn a golden red. A few fallen leaves already dot the grass underneath it.

"I think we should put it right about there," says Ms. Moses, gesturing with her free hand. Reggie's birdhouse is tucked firmly under her other arm. He stained the wood so that it's a natural-looking brown—it almost matches the shade of the tree trunk—and fashioned old tin scraps from his garage into a roof. I helped him outline an intricate pattern of vines around the three sides of the opening that functions as the door, and he painted the vines a dark forest green.

Katie, Missy, and Rachel keep walking, but I stay to watch as Ms. Moses inches up a ladder that's leaning against the tree.

"How about this?" she asks.

"It's your work, Mr. Walker," says Mrs. Schein.

"That looks like a good spot," Reggie says. "What do you think, Violet?"

I move closer to him.

"Looks good to me," I say.

Katie turns back and stops to wait for me.

"Violet, aren't you coming? I thought we were going to play four square," she says, and then she holds up the ball as evidence of our plan.

"In a minute."

"What do you think?" Reggie asks Katie as he points to the tree.

Ever since the bee incident, it's like an outside layer of himself got rubbed off, and Reggie's more open to talking to other people. When he came back to school, he started sitting with us at lunch, and we found out that he and Katie actually have something in common. Katie knows a little about birds because her grandfather's taken her bird-watching.

"Is that a birdhouse?" asks Katie as she joins us by the tree.

"I built it for art," Reggie says.

"Wow. It's so cool," Katie says.

"C'mon, Katie, let's go play four square," Missy says impatiently.

"You go ahead without me," Katie says, handing Missy the ball.

"When are you guys coming?" asks Rachel. "We're going to need to find substitutes until then."

"Find somebody else to take my place. I'm going to stay here," I say.

"Me too," says Katie.

"Really?" asks Rachel.

"Forget it," says Missy. She shakes her head at us and walks away quickly, as though she saw something unpleasant. Rachel shrugs and then runs after her—toes facing straight out, like a duck out of water.

"Look!" Katie says.

She points to a bird with a long, slender beak that's perched on a high branch, way above the spot for Reggie's house. Its body is a warm brown flecked with even darker spots. There's one bright orange mark on its head.

"It's so beautiful," I say.

"It's a type of woodpecker called a northern flicker," Reggie explains. "I've seen one before in the tree in front of the school."

"Maybe it's looking for a home," says Katie. "I know! It can take its family and move into your birdhouse."

"No," says Reggie firmly. "I don't think it would do that. Most woodpeckers live alone unless they're breeding."

"Aww," says Katie. "That's so sad."

I think Katie's right. I hate to picture these birds out there alone in the world.

"If that's how they live, then they must not need any-thing else," says Mrs. Schein. "They must be able to survive that way."

"Just because they *can* survive alone doesn't mean they *should*," I say.

Right after I say it, I feel embarrassed to have contradicted Mrs. Schein. I hope she doesn't think I'm being rude and give me detention.

Instead of being annoyed, Mrs. Schein nods.

"You know what, Ms. Crane? That's true."

"Yeah, poor flicker. He's really missing out," Reggie says.

"Well, at least you're giving him a home. That's a good place to start," says Mrs. Schein. "And what about you, Ms. Crane? I hear from Mr. Walker that he's helping you build your own birdhouse."

"He is," I say. "We've worked on it at my house every day this week."

"Cool. Does yours look the same?" asks Katie.

"Not exactly. It's made out of a different kind of wood—from an old project that Reggie and I took apart. You could come over to my house today, too. We could always use more help, right?" I say to Reggie.

"Sure," says Reggie.

"Won't your mom mind because she'll be busy with work?" asks Katie.

"She won't mind."

"If the three of us work together, we should finish it in no time," Reggie says. "Then we can put your house here in this tree, next to mine. Just like at home," Reggie says to me.

"I wish I had a good friend who lived right next door to me," says Katie.

"Our houses our close enough that we can practically see each other through the windows," explains Reggie.

"You guys are lucky," says Katie.

"Yeah," I say. "We really are."